喚醒你的英文語感！

Get a Feel for English !

喚醒你的英文語感 ！

Get a Feel for English !

搞定 *Receiving Guests*
接待英文

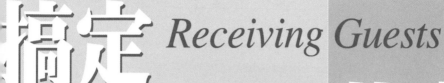

際商務夥伴來訪，要建立穩固交情，只有安排接機
食宿恐怕不夠，如何接待得宜，親伴參訪在地遊，
合作關係挹注養份，本書幫你搞定！

16 個接待最常見情境
32 個擬真對話範例
388 個拉近距離好用句
250 個招待在地遊加分字彙

附 2 片實戰CD

總編審⊙王復國
作　者⊙Jason Grenier

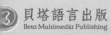

貝塔語言出版
Beta Multimedia Publishing

PREFACE

Have you ever heard or seen an English word or phrase, and then thought to yourself, "I know that word! I've seen it before, but... I just can't remember it!" If you have, it probably means that you don't really "know" that word yet, you've just "encountered" it. It may have been in your short-term memory for a while, but now it's gone!

Most of us, when we encounter a new word or phrase, look the phrase up in a dictionary, and then repeat it to ourselves several times in an attempt to memorize it. This approach is largely ineffective. Language experts say that we need to be exposed to a new word or phrase at least five times—in different contexts—before we will be able to remember it, and before it will go into our long-term memory.

The late Dr. Paul Pimsleur, one of the world's leading experts in applied linguistics, developed a theory to explain this phenomenon, which he called "Graduated Interval Recall." This theory says that target words and phrases need to be introduced at periodic intervals for them to move from short-term into long-term memory. Dr. Pimsleur also advocated mastering the "Core Vocabulary" of any language—those words and phrases that occur most frequently, and which form the foundation of language proficiency.

Beta's Biz English series was designed with Pimsleur's theories about language and memory in mind. In this book on receiving guests, readers are taught the 388 core phrases for receiving guests. Each phrase is introduced once, along with a sample sentence. Then, many of the phrases are repeated again in the "Show Time" dialogue in each chapter, where readers can see how the phrase is used in a larger context.

It's often said that "repetition is the mother of mastery," and there is no area where this is more true than in learning a foreign language. Devote yourself to studying the content in this book, and to listening to the accompanying CDs, and you won't just have encountered the material, you'll have really learned it.

Happy Studying,

Mark Hammons

英文主編序

你有沒有曾經聽到或看到某個英文單字或用語，然後心裡想：「我認識這個單字！我看過，可是……我就是記不起來！」如果你有這種經驗，就表示你還沒真正「認識」這個字，你只是曾經「遇見」它。也許這個字存在你的短期記憶裡有那麼一下子，不過現在卻煙消雲散了。

遇到新的單字或用語時，我們大部分的人會查字典，然後複誦個幾遍試圖背起來，但這種方法的效果十分有限。語言專家指出，我們要在不同語境中接觸到一個字或詞至少五次才能把它們記起來，我們的長期記憶也才能加以儲存。

已故的保羅・皮姆斯勒博士是全球應用語言學界的翹楚，他發展出一種理論來解釋此現象，他稱之為「漸進式間歇回想」。這種理論認為目標單字或用語必須經過週期性間隔導入，才能從短期記憶化為長期記憶。皮姆斯勒博士也提倡熟悉任一語言裡的「核心字庫」，也就是最常被使用、構成精通該語言基礎的字詞。

貝塔的商用英文書系是依皮姆斯勒博士針對語言和記憶的理論設計而成。在這本接待英文的書籍裡，讀者會學到 388 個接待客戶所需的核心句型。每種句型會附一個例句呈現，而其中許多句型會在每章「Show Time」對話單元中重複出現，這時候讀者能夠領略如何把這類句型用在更廣的語境中。

常有人說「反覆能造就精通」，這句話用在學習外語方面再正確也不過了。希望你能全心吸收本書內容，並認真聆聽搭配的CD，你將不只是與教材內容匆匆交會，而是實實在在學會了。

祝各位學習愉快。

Mark Hammons

CONTENTS

第 **1** 章

接機
At the Airport

As part of doing business in the global village, you have to be prepared to look after overseas clients who are in town for business, ensuring that the foreigners have a comfortable and pleasant stay. Your work can start as soon as your client steps off the plane with the "meet and greet" at the airport. This is an important moment, as favorable first impressions go a long way. It's a big responsibility, but with the right vocabulary, you'll be up to the challenge.

在地球村做生意，你必須隨時準備好招待前來商務拜訪的國外客戶，確保外國友人在停留期間能感到舒適、愉快，這是工作的一部分。客戶步出機門後，雙方在機場「見面致意」那刻起，就是工作的開始。這是重要的一刻，因為好的開始就是成功的一半；這個責任十分重大，但只要說對話，你就能從容應戰。

1 Biz 必通句型 Need-to-Know Phrases

 CD I-02

1.1 竭誠歡迎 Welcoming

當訪客蒞臨後，你可以用下列這三句話來迎接他們。

❶ **Hello!.... Welcome to.... My name is....**
您好！……。歡迎來……，我是……。
例 Hello! Mr. Matthews. Welcome to Taipei. My name is Lawrence Chen.
您好！馬修士先生。歡迎來台北，我是勞倫斯・陳。

❷ **How was your...?**
您的……還好嗎？
例 How was your flight?
您這趟飛行還好嗎？

❸ **You must be tired after such....**
在這樣的……後，您一定累了。
例 It's a long way from Sydney. You must be tired after such a long journey.
從雪梨到這裡路途遙遠。在這樣的長途旅行後，您一定累了。

幾句寒喧之後，接著就要帶客戶離開機場。

❹ **There's a... waiting for us (location).**
（地點）有……在等我們。
例 There's a car and driver waiting for us outside the <u>terminal</u>. The driver will take us directly to your hotel.
航站外面有車子和司機在等我們，司機會直接送您去您下榻的飯店。

❺ My car is parked....

我的車停在……。

例 My car is parked in the <u>Departures</u> <u>lot</u>. It's not far.

我的車停在出站區，離這裡不遠。

❻ Please follow me. The... is this way.

請跟我來，……在這邊。

例 Please follow me, Mr. Matthews. The car is this way.

請跟我來，馬修士先生。車子在這邊。

如果你的客人行李很多，最好找輛手推車，這樣你們才不會手忙腳亂。

❼ Can I help you with your...?

我幫您拿……好嗎？

例 Can I help you with your golf <u>clubs</u>? They must be heavy.

我幫您拿高爾夫球具好嗎？它們一定很重。

❽ We can put your... in the trunk.

我們可以把您的……放進行李箱。

例 We can put your golf clubs in the trunk. It will be more comfortable that way.

我們可以把您的高爾夫球具放進行李箱，這樣會舒適一點。

 Word List

terminal [ˋtɝmən!] *n.* 航廈；飛機、船隻、火車及巴士的起始終點站

departure [dɪˋpɑrtʃɚ] *n.* 離開；出發；啟程

lot [lɑt] *n.* 一塊地；籤

club [klʌb] *n.* （高爾夫）球桿

1.2 上車／計程車後 In the Car/Taxi

最好告訴客人你們要去的地方，不要認為他／她已經知道。

❶ Would you like to go directly to the..., or is there anywhere you'd like to stop <u>along</u> the way?
您想直接到……，還是沿途有什麼地方您想去？
例 Would you like to go directly to the factory, Mr. Matthews, or is there anywhere you'd like to stop along the way?
馬修士先生，您想直接到工廠，還是沿途有什麼地方您想去？

長途旅行後的客人聽了下列這三句話應該會感覺比較輕鬆。

❷ We should be at the... in about... minutes.
再……分鐘左右我們應該就會到……。
例 We should be at the office in about 25 minutes, so long as the traffic isn't too heavy.
只要路上不塞車，再 25 分鐘左右我們應該就會到辦公室。

❸ The traffic (shouldn't be/<u>is bound to</u> be) heavy at this time of (day/night).
（白天／晚上）這個時間（應該不會／一定會）塞車。
例 The traffic shouldn't be heavy at this time of night.
晚上這個時間應該不會塞車。

❹ Is this your first time in...?
這是您第一次來……？
例 Is this your first time in Taiwan?
這是您第一次來台灣嗎？

Word List
....
along [ə`lɔŋ] *prep.* 沿著；順著   be bound to V. 一定會……

不妨當個導遊帶客人認識一下城市及環境特色，下列這三句話能派上用場。

❺ As you can see,... is a(n) (adj.) city.

如您所見，……是個（形容詞）的城市。

例 As you can see, Beijing is a rapidly <u>modernizing</u> city. There's an amazing amount of construction going on.

如您所見，北京是個急遽現代化的城市，正在進行的工程數量多得驚人。

❻ To our (right/left) you can see....

在我們的（右邊／左邊），您可以看到……。

例 To our right you can see the Shinkong Mitsukoshi Tower. It's one of the tallest <u>skyscrapers</u> in the city.

在我們的右邊，您可以看到新光三越大樓。這是市內數一數二高的摩天大樓。

❼ We're coming up on....

我們即將來到……。

例 We're coming up on the <u>garment</u> <u>district</u>. This is where most of the city's tailor shops, <u>fabric</u> suppliers, and clothing <u>manufacturers</u> are located.

我們即將來到成衣區。市內大部分的裁縫店、布料供應商和成衣製造商都聚集在此地。

用下面這句話來讓客人知道，你們已經抵達目的地。

❽ Here we are, (name of guest), (name of place).

我們到了，（客人的名字），這裡是（地名）。

例 Here we are, Mr. Matthews, the Evergreen Hotel. Let's get you checked in.

我們到了，馬修士先生，這裡就是長榮酒店。我們去辦理您的住宿手續。

Ｗord List

modernizing [`mɑdən͵aɪzɪŋ] *adj.* 現代化的

skyscraper [`skaɪ͵skrepɚ] *n.* 摩天大廈

garment [`gɑrmənt] *n.* 成衣

district [`dɪstrɪkt] *n.* 區；地帶

fabric [`fæbrɪk] *n.* 布料

manufacturer [͵mænjə`fæktʃərɚ] *n.* 製造商

2 實戰會話 Show Time

2.1 At the Airport

CD I-03

Terry Matthews is an important <u>client</u> of Trenix Systems in Taiwan. John Liu works at Trenix and is responsible for <u>receiving</u> him. They meet in Beijing for an international <u>exposition</u> and will travel to Taiwan together after the exposition.

John: Hello! Mr. Matthews. Welcome to Beijing. My name is John Liu.

Terry: Hi, John. How are you doing?

John: I'm just fine, thanks. How was your flight?

Terry: Not bad. <u>Smooth</u> sailing all the way, but long enough for <u>my liking</u>.

John: I can imagine. You must be tired after such a long journey. But not to worry—there's a taxi waiting for us outside the terminal. We'll get you to your hotel <u>in no time</u>.

Terry: Great, thanks. I'll feel much better once I get <u>freshened up</u>.

John: Of course. Please follow me, Mr. Matthews. The taxi <u>stand</u> is this way. Can I help you with your bags?

Terry: That's OK, thanks John. I can <u>manage</u>. I always travel light when I'm on business.

譯文

在機場

約翰‧馬修士是台灣川尼斯系統公司的一個重要客戶,約翰‧劉在川尼斯工作並且負責接待他。他們在北京碰面參加一場國際展覽會,展覽之後他們會一起到台灣。

約翰:您好!馬修士先生。歡迎來北京,我是約翰‧劉。

泰瑞:嗨,約翰。你好嗎?

約翰:我很好,謝謝。您這趟飛行還好嗎?

泰瑞:還不錯,一路平順,只是飛行時數有點太長了。

約翰:我能想像。在這樣的長途旅行後,您一定累了。不過別擔心,有輛計程車在航站外面等我們,我們馬上就送您到飯店。

泰瑞:太好了,謝謝。我梳洗一下就會覺得好多了。

約翰:當然。請跟我來,馬修士先生。計程車站在這邊。我幫您拿袋子好嗎?

泰瑞:沒關係,謝了,約翰。我拿得動。外出商務旅遊時我總是輕裝便行。

Word List

client [`klaɪənt] *n.* 顧客;客戶;委託人
receive [rɪ`siv] *v.* 接待;得到;收到
exposition [ˌɛkspə`zɪʃən] *n.* (=expo) 展覽會;博覽會
smooth [smuð] *adj.* 平滑的;順利的
something is too... for someone's liking 某事物太……某人不喜歡(liking [`laɪkɪŋ] *n.* 喜歡;愛好)
in no time 立刻;很快
freshen up [ˌfrɛʃən `ʌp] *phr. v.* 梳洗;使……煥然一新
stand [stænd] *n.* 計程車、公車的招呼站
manage [`mænɪʤ] *v.* 處理;經營;管理

2.2 From the Airport to the Hotel

In the taxi.

John: Would you like to go directly to the hotel, Mr. Matthews, or is there anywhere you'd like to stop along the way?

Terry: <u>Straight</u> to the hotel if you don't mind—I'm really <u>beat</u>.

John: No problem—we should be at the hotel in about 20 minutes. The traffic shouldn't be heavy at this time of night. So, is this your first time in Beijing?

Terry: Yep, first time.

John: As you can see, Beijing is a huge city. The total area is more than 16,800 <u>square kilometers,</u> including the suburbs.

Terry: Wow! That's unbelievable.

John: To our right you can see some of the construction that's going on to prepare for <u>the</u> 2008 <u>Olympics</u>.

Terry: Very <u>impressive</u>! I guess the next four years will see a lot of changes. The eyes of the world are going to be on Beijing.

John: Definitely. It's an exciting time for the city. Here we are, Mr. Matthews, the Lotus Hotel.

從機場到飯店

上計程車後

約翰：馬修士先生，您想直接到飯店，還是沿途有什麼地方您想去？

泰瑞：直接去飯店，如果你不介意的話——我實在累慘了。

約翰：沒問題——再 20 分鐘左右我們應該就會到飯店，晚上這個時間應該不會塞車。那，這是您第一次來北京嗎？

泰瑞：是的，第一次來。

約翰：如您所見，北京是個大都市。包括郊區在內，總面積超過一萬六千八百平方公里。

泰瑞：哇！難以置信。

約翰：在我們的右邊，您可以看到有一些工程正在進行，這是為了準備 2008 年的奧運。

泰瑞：非常令人印象深刻！我想未來四年內會看到很多變化，北京將會是全世界矚目的焦點。

約翰：肯定是。對這個城市來說，這是令人興奮的時刻。我們到了，馬修士先生，這裡就是蓮花酒店。

Word List

straight [stret] *adv.* 直接地

beat [bit] *adj.* （口語）筋疲力盡的

square kilometers [`skwɛr kɪ`ləmətəz] *n.* 平方公里

the Olympics [ðə o`lɪmpɪks] *n.* (= the Olympic Games) 奧運

impressive [ɪm`prɛsɪv] *adj.* 令人印象深刻的

definitely [`dɛfənɪtlɪ] *adv.* 一定；明確地

3 Biz 加分句型 Nice-to-Know Phrases

 CD I-04

3.1 辨識客人 <u>Recognizing</u> Your Guests

❶ Excuse me. Are you...?
對不起，請問您是……嗎？
例 Excuse me. Are you Mr. Black?
　　對不起，請問您是布雷克先生嗎？

❷ You must be....
您一定就是……。
例 You must be Ms. Portman.
　　您一定就是波曼小姐。

❸ You don't happen to be..., do you?
您不會就是……，是嗎？
例 You don't happen to be Mrs. Sears, do you?
　　您不會就是席爾斯太太，是嗎？

❹ I hope you <u>haven't been waiting</u> long.（找到對的人之後說）
希望沒讓您久等。
例 Sorry, Mr. Hatton, I <u>wasn't aware</u> your flight arrived early. I hope you haven't been waiting long.
　　抱歉，哈登先生，我不知道您的班機早到，希望沒讓您久等。

ord List

recognize [ˋrɛkəgˌnaɪz] v. 認出；識別
have been V-ing 一直在……（現在完成進行式，表示動作持續進行）
be aware (that) 子句, be aware of sth. 意識到……；知道……

3.2 客人旅途不順 Your Guest Has a Bad Flight

旅行（尤其是長途旅行）不順遂是一件令人生氣又無奈的事，你的安慰
多少能幫助客戶分擔一些情緒。

❶ That sounds....（聽完客人抱怨後，表示理解與同情）
聽起來⋯⋯。
例 That sounds terrible. I can imagine.
聽起來真糟，我能想像。

❷ I'm sorry you had....（表示遺憾）
很遺憾您⋯⋯。
例 I'm sorry you had such an unpleasant flight.
很遺憾您有一段這麼不愉快的航程。

聽了下列這兩句話，客人應該會感覺窩心。

❸ We really appreciate....（感謝客人前來）
我們十分感謝⋯⋯。
例 We really appreciate you coming all this way.
我們十分感謝您不遠千里而來。

❹ We're so glad that....（尤其當客人是從遠地來時）
我們非常高興⋯⋯。
例 We're so glad that you made the time to come talk in person.
我們非常高興您抽空親自前來商談。

Ⓦord List
⋯⋯⋯⋯⋯⋯⋯⋯⋯⋯⋯⋯⋯⋯⋯⋯⋯⋯⋯⋯⋯⋯⋯⋯⋯⋯⋯⋯⋯⋯
appreciate [ə`priʃɪˌet] *v.* 感激；欣賞；賞識
in person 親自

4 Biz 加分字彙 Nice-to-Know Vocabulary

 CD I-05

❶ airline [ˋɛrˏlaɪn] *n.* 航空公司；（飛機的）航線

❷ arrival [əˋraɪvl] *n.* 抵達

❸ origin [ˋɔrədʒɪn] *n.* 出發地

❹ destination [ˏdɛstəˋneʃən] *n.* 目的地

❺ flight number [ˋflaɪt ˏnʌmbɚ] *n.* 航班號碼

❻ customs [ˋkʌstəmz] *n.*（複數形）海關；關稅

❼ immigration [ˏɪməˋgreʃən] *n.* 入境；移入某地

❽ layover [ˋleˏovɚ] *n.* 旅程中途停留（如轉機等所做的停靠）

❾ flight attendant [ˋflaɪt əˋtɛndənt] *n.* 空服員

❿ baggage claim [ˋbægɪdʒ ˏklem] *n.* 行李提領區

⓫ cart [kɑrt] *n.* 手推車

⓬ currency exchange [ˋkɝənsɪ ɪksˋtʃendʒ] *n.* 貨幣兌換

⓭ cellphone rental [ˋsɛlfon ˏrɛntl] *n.* 行動電話出租

⓮ car rental [ˋkɑr ˏrɛntl] *n.* 租車；租車服務

⓯ deposit [dɪˋpɑzɪt] *n.* 押金；訂金

┊┊┊┊┊┊┊ 小心陷阱 ┊┊┊┊┊┊┊

☹ 錯誤用法

The traffic shouldn't be very much.

應該不會太塞車。

☺ 正確用法

There shouldn't be too much traffic.

應該不會太塞車。

┊┊┊┊┊┊┊ 文化小叮嚀 ┊┊┊┊┊┊┊

After a long flight, people are usually tired and they may even be a little bit <u>irritable</u>. When you offer to help a guest with their bags, take a NO answer as a NO. Asking "Are you sure?" to <u>ensure</u> the guest is not just being overly polite is OK. <u>Insisting on</u> helping is not. A <u>tug-of-war</u> over a suitcase in the airport is a bad start to any business relationship.

長途飛行之後，人們通常相當疲倦，有時甚至有些焦躁易怒。當你表示要幫客人提袋子時，客人說「不用」就應該視為「不用」。問一句「真的不用嗎？」，來確定客人並非因為太客氣而拒絕尚無礙，但堅持幫忙就不妥。不管是哪種商業關係，在機場上演一場手提箱爭奪戰都不是個好的開始。

ord List

irritiable [ˈɪrətəbl] *adj.* 易惱怒的；焦躁的

ensure [ɪnˈʃur] *v.* 使確定；確保

insist on N./V-ing, insist that 子句 堅持……

tug-of-war [ˈtʌɡəv ˈwɔr] *n.* 拔河；爭奪戰

5 實戰演練 Practice Exercises

I 請為下列三題選出最適本章的中文譯義。

❶ go on

(A) 發生 (B) 持續進行 (C) 接著⋯⋯

❷ come up

(A) 上來 (B) 出現 (C) 靠近

❸ in no time

(A) 沒有時間 (B) 立刻 (C) 準時

II 你會如何回應下面這兩句話？

❶ I'll feel much better once I get freshened up.

(A) Yes, there's nothing worse than being stale.

(B) There's a restroom over there—take your time.

(C) Please do something about that body odor.

❷ I'm really beat!

(A) Yeah, you look like someone punched you in the face.

(B) I always win at chess.

(C) Why don't you go back to the hotel and take a nap?

III 你開車載成衣零售連鎖店的採購，緹娜·徐，去你們市中心的辦公室。緹娜說想趁在這裡的期間拍一些著名建築景點的照片，你想給她這個機會。請利用下列詞語寫出一篇簡短的對話：

we're coming up on	old City Hall	stop along the way
take pictures	go directly to	

＊解答請見 226 頁

第**2**章

飯店
At the Hotel

A hotel will likely be home away from home for your guests while they are in town. As a good host, you must ensure that they are checked in and comfortable.

當客人來訪時，飯店對他們而言就是在外地的家。作為盡職的東道，你必須確定他們順利登記入宿而且住得舒適。

1 Biz 必通句型 Need-to-Know Phrases

CD I-06

1.1 討論飯店 Discussing the Hotel

如果你想讓客人覺得你幫忙挑了一家不錯的飯店，下列這句話可以幫助你達到目的。

❶ The (name) Hotel has a <u>reputation</u> for....
（名稱）飯店以……著稱。
例 The Evergreen Hotel has a reputation for excellent service.
長榮酒店以卓越的服務著稱。

不妨讓客人知道你安排了哪種房間，這樣，如果有必要的話，他們才能要求換房。

❷ We've already <u>reserved</u> you a....
我們已經幫您訂了一間……。
例 We've already reserved you a suite.
我們已經幫您訂了一間套房。

❸ Let's get you checked in so you can....
我們去辦理您的住宿手續，好讓您……。
例 Let's get you checked in so you can take a rest.
我們去辦理您的住宿手續，好讓您休息一下。

❹ Do you prefer a... room?
您較喜歡……房嗎？
例 Do you prefer a smoking or a non-smoking room?
您較喜歡吸菸房還是禁菸房？

ord List

reputation [ˌrɛpjə`teʃən] *n.* 名聲 (have a reputation for= have a name for)
reserve [rɪ`zɝv] *v.* 預訂；保留

❺ I believe (location) has/have <u>wireless</u> Internet access.

我想（地點）可以無線上網。

例 I believe the lobby has wireless Internet <u>access</u>.

我想大廳可以無線上網。

❻ This hotel (or hotel name) is very popular with....

這家飯店（或飯店名稱）頗受⋯⋯的歡迎。

例 This hotel is very popular with foreign visitors.

這家飯店頗受外國客人的歡迎。

幫客人辦好住宿手續後，你可以跟他們介紹一下飯店的其他服務。

❼ This hotel has all the <u>amenities</u>—there's....

這家飯店的設施一應俱全——有⋯⋯。

例 This hotel has all the amenities—there's a gym, a pool, and a sauna in the basement level.

這家飯店的設施一應俱全——地下樓層有健身房、游泳池及蒸氣室。

❽ Would you like me to <u>arrange</u> for...?

您需要我幫忙安排⋯⋯嗎？

例 Would you like me to arrange for laundry or dry-cleaning service?

您需要我幫忙安排送洗或乾洗服務嗎？

Ｗord List

wireless [ˋwaɪrlɪs] *adj.* 無線的（無線上網 Wireless Internet Access 利用無線區域網路 Wireless Local Area Network[WLAN]以無線訊號的方式傳送資料，使用者需將無線網卡 WLAN Card 插入 PDA、筆記型電腦等內，經由無線帳號及基地台連接上線）

access [ˋæksɛs] *n.* 可取得⋯⋯的管道（access to sth. 獲得某事物的管道）

amenities [əˋminətɪz] *n.* （常用複數）便利設施；福利設施

arrange [əˋrendʒ] *v.* 安排；籌備

1.2 約定後續的會面 Making Plans to <u>Meet up</u> Later

跟客人說清楚什麼時候會再見面是很重要的。

❶ **Let's meet (location) at (time).**
我們（時間）在（地點）碰面。
例 Lets meet in the coffee shop at eleven-thirty.
我們十一點半在咖啡店碰面。

❷ **(Event) is at (time), so I'll meet you (location) at (time), alright?**
（活動）是在（時間），所以我們（時間）在（地點）碰面，可以嗎？
例 Our <u>tee-off</u> time is at nine o'clock tomorrow, so I'll meet you here at eight-fifteen, alright?
我們開球的時間是在明天早上九點，所以我們八點十五在這裡碰面，可以嗎？

由於你不可能一直陪在客人身邊，不妨讓他們知道還有哪些資源可使用。

❸ **You can ask at the front desk—they'll arrange for....**
您可以問櫃台──他們會幫忙安排……。
例 You can ask at the front desk—they'll arrange for a taxi.
您可以問櫃台──他們會幫您叫計程車。

適時遞上名片不僅有助加深客人對你的印象，還是他們請求援助的最佳工具。

Ⓦord List

meet up [`mit ˌʌp] *phr. v.* （安排好的）見面；（不期然的）遇到
tee-off [ˌti`ɔf] *adj./n.* 高爾夫球起桿發球（tee 為插在土裡置放高爾夫球的球座）

❹ You can just give this card to the.... The address is printed on it in (language).

您只要把這張名片拿給……就好了，上面印有（語言）地址。

例 You can just give this card to the taxi driver. The address is printed on it in Chinese.

您只要把這張名片拿給計程車司機就好了，上面印有中文地址。

❺ There will be a car and driver waiting for you at (time).

（時間）會有車子和司機等著接您。

例 There will be a car and driver waiting for you at eight o'clock tomorrow morning.

明天早上八點會有車子和司機等著接您。

在你離開之前，應該問一下客人是否還需要任何協助。

❻ Looks like you're....

看來您好像……。

例 Looks like you're all set.

看來您好像都準備好了。

❼ Is there anything else I can do for you before...?

在……之前，還有什麼忙我可以幫的嗎？

例 Is there anything else I can do for you before I go?

在我告辭之前，還有什麼我可以幫忙的嗎？

別忘了！離開前的祝福是種禮貌。

❽ Have a nice...,.... See you....

祝您有個美好的……，……。……見。

例 Have a nice evening, Mr. Stevenson. See you tomorrow.

祝您有個美好的夜晚，史帝文森先生。明天見。

2 實戰會話 Show Time

2.1 Checking In

John and Terry are walking into the lobby of the hotel where Terry will be staying. His company has already made a reservation for him, but John wants to ensure that everything goes smoothly.

John: The Lotus Hotel—very nice! The Lotus has a reputation for some of the best views of the city <u>skyline</u>.

Terry: Yeah, another sales <u>rep</u> from the company stayed here once. He said the same thing.

John: I'm not surprised—the Lotus is very popular with business people. Let's get you checked in so you can get freshened up before the <u>banquet</u>.

Terry: I hear that! I'm looking forward to that shower and a change of clothes.

John is talking to Terry while the desk clerk deals with the check-in <u>procedures</u>, credit card, etc.

John: The Lotus has all the amenities—there's a business center and they even offer <u>secretarial</u> service, for a price, of course.

Terry: I don't think I'll need it, but it's good to know it's available if I do.

John: Would you like me to arrange for a wake-up call?

Terry: No thanks, John—no need. I brought my <u>trusty</u> travel alarm clock!

譯 文

辦理住宿手續

約翰和泰瑞正走進泰瑞所要留宿的飯店大廳，他的公司已經幫他訂好房間，但約翰想確定一切都沒問題。

約翰：蓮花飯店──太棒了！蓮花以能眺見本市最棒的一些天際建築輪廓著稱。

泰瑞：是啊，公司另一個業務代表住過這裡，他也這麼說。

約翰：我不驚訝──蓮花頗受商務人士的歡迎。我們去辦理您的住宿手續，好讓您可以在宴會開始之前梳洗一下。

泰瑞：太好了！我好期待洗那個澡及換衣服。

在櫃台人員處理住宿手續和信用卡等的同時，約翰跟泰瑞繼續說話。

約翰：蓮花的設施一應俱全──有商務中心，他們甚至還提供祕書服務；當然，那是需要付費的。

泰瑞：我想我用不到，不過知道需要時有得用感覺蠻好的。

約翰：您需要我幫忙安排電話鬧鈴嗎？

泰瑞：不，謝了，約翰──不需要。我自己帶了可靠的旅行鬧鐘！

Word List

skyline [ˋskaɪˌlaɪn] *n.* 以天空為背景遠眺建築物所見的輪廓、線條
rep [rɛp] *n.* （非正式）代表（=representative）
banquet [ˋbæŋkwɪt] *n.* 宴會；盛宴
procedure [prəˋsidʒɚ] *n.* 手續；行事規則；步驟
secretarial [ˌsɛkrəˋtɛrɪəl] *adj.* 秘書的
trusty [ˋtrʌstɪ] *adj.* 值得信賴的（可形容東西、動物及人）

2.2 Saying Goodbye at the Hotel

Terry has finished checking in—he has his room key, and he's ready to go upstairs. It's time for John to go, but before he does, he and Terry must make <u>arrangements</u> to meet up later to attend a banquet.

Terry: Tell me again—what time is the banquet?

John: The banquet is at 8:00, so I'll meet you here in the lobby at 7:30, all right?

Terry: Will that give us enough time?

John: Yes, plenty. The banquet hall is quite close by.

Terry: Sounds like a plan, then.

John: Looks like you're all <u>set up</u> here. Is there anything else I can do for you before I leave?

Terry: No, thanks, John. You've been a big help.

John: It's my pleasure. See you at seven-thirty.

在飯店道別

泰瑞辦好了住宿手續——他拿到房間鑰匙，準備好上樓。約翰差不多該離開了，但在離開之前，他和泰瑞必須先約好稍後見面去參加宴會。

泰瑞：再提醒我一次——宴會是幾點？

約翰：宴會在八點，所以我七點半跟您在大廳碰面，可以嗎？

泰瑞：這樣我們時間夠嗎？

約翰：夠，綽綽有餘。宴會廳離這裡很近。

泰瑞：聽起來一切都計劃地很妥當。

約翰：看來您這裡一切就緒。在我告辭之前，還有什麼我可以幫忙的嗎？

泰瑞：沒有了，謝謝你，約翰。你幫了非常多的忙。

約翰：這是我的榮幸。我們七點半見。

ord List

arrangement [əˋrendʒmənts] *n.* （通常複數）安排；準備工作
set up [ˏsɛt ˋʌp] *phr. v.* 計劃籌備；創立

3 Biz 加分句型 Nice-to-Know Phrases

 CD I-08

3.1 留客人在飯店 Leaving Guests at the Hotel

❶ I hope you'll have a/an (adj.) stay.

希望您住得（形容詞）。

例 I hope you'll have a comfortable stay.

希望您住得舒適。

❷ All/Most of the staff here speaks (language), so....

這裡所有／大部分的員工都會講（語言），所以⋯⋯。

例 Most of the staff here speaks English, so you shouldn't have any problems.

這裡大部分的員工都會講英文，所以您應該不會有什麼問題。

❸ If you need....

如果您需要⋯⋯。

例 If you need anything at all, just call me.

假如您有任何需要，打個電話給我就行了。

❹ I have... with me <u>at all times</u>, so....

我總是帶著⋯⋯，所以⋯⋯。

例 I have my cell phone with me at all times, so call me if you need anything.

我總是帶著手機，所以如果您有任何需要的話，打電話給我。

ord List

at all times 總是

3.2 處理對飯店的抱怨 Dealing with Hotel Complaints

如果客人説不想住已經訂好的那間飯店，你應該如何處理？

❶ Not to worry. I'd be happy to....
請不用擔心，我很樂意……。
例 Not to worry. I'd be happy to take you to another hotel.
請不用擔心，我很樂意帶您去另一家飯店。

❷ There are several... that I can recommend.
有幾家……我可以推薦。
例 There are several good hotels in town that I can recommend.
市區還有幾家不錯的飯店我可以推薦。

❸ If you prefer, I can....
如果您比較喜歡的話，我可以……。
例 If you prefer, I can take you to a different hotel.
如果您希望的話，我可以帶您去另一家飯店。

如果客人只是稍微抱怨之前的住宿經驗，下面這句話可以讓他們放心一點。

❹ Don't worry—I'll talk to....
別擔心——我會跟……說。
例 Don't worry—I'll talk to the <u>concierge</u> and make sure that doesn't happen this time.
別擔心——我會關照櫃檯人員以確保這次不會再發生同樣的事。

Word List

concierge [kɑnsɪ`ɛrʒ] *n.* 門房；旅館服務台職員

4 Biz 加分字彙 Nice-to-Know Vocabulary

CD I-09

1. deluxe room [dɪ`lʌks `rum] *n.* 豪華客房
2. superior room [sə`pɪrɪɚ `rum] *n.* 精緻客房
3. executive room [ɪg`zɛkjʊtɪv `rum] *n.* 行政客房
4. presidential suite [`prɛzədɛnʃəl `swit] *n.* 總統套房
5. iron [`aɪɚn] *n.* 熨斗；ironing board [`aɪɚnɪŋ ˏbord] *n.* 燙衣板
6. bathtub [`bæθˏtʌb] *n.* 浴缸
7. satellite television [`sætḷˏaɪt `tɛləˏvɪʒən] *n.* 衛星電視
8. safety deposit box [`seftɪ dɪ`pɑzɪt `bɑks] *n.* 保險箱
9. direct phone [dəˏrɛkt `fon] *n.* 直播電話
10. air conditioning [`ɛr kənˏdɪʃənɪŋ] *n.* 空調系統
11. florist [`florɪst] *n.* 花店；花商
12. laundromat [`lɑndrəmæt] *n.* 自助洗衣店
13. luggage storage [`lʌgɪdʒ `storɪdʒ] *n.* 行李寄放
14. babysitting service [`bebɪsɪtɪŋ `sɝvɪs] *n.* 褓姆服務
15. valet parking [`vælɪt ˏpɑrkɪŋ] *n.* 代客泊車

┌──────── 小心陷阱 ────────┐

☹ 錯誤用法：

This hotel is **high-class**.

這是家一流的飯店。

☺ 正確用法：

This is a **first-class** hotel.

這是家一流的飯店。

└────────────────────────┘

┌──────── 文化小叮嚀 ────────┐

If you live in a country where it's not uncommon for hotel staff to enter a guest's room without <u>knocking</u>, <u>warn</u> your guest <u>about</u> this, and <u>remind</u> them to lock their room door to prevent an unwelcome <u>intrusion</u>.

如果你所居住的國家，飯店人員經常不敲門就進入客人的房間的話，最好預告你的客人這點，並提醒他們將房門上鎖，以避免不期然的「拜訪」。

└────────────────────────┘

ord List

knock [nɑk] *v.* 敲；擊

warn sb. about sth. 警告某人某事

remind [rɪ`maɪnd] *v.* 提醒；使想起

intrusion [ɪn`truʒən] *n.* 闖入；干擾

5 實戰演練 Practice Exercises

I 請為下列三題選出最適本章的中文譯義。

1 make arrangements

(A) 規劃安排 (B) 協商解決 (C) 裝飾佈置

2 set up

(A) 設計陷害 (B) 成立 (C) 安排準備

3 Sounds like a plan.

(A) 聽起來好像都計劃好了！ (B) 聽起來像個計謀！ (C) 聽起來是個目標！

II 你會如何回應下面這兩句話？

1 Looks like you're all set.

(A) Yes, it's quite a surprise to me too.

(B) Yes, I have everything I need.

(C) Yes, I can barely move.

2 Last time I stayed at this hotel, they were vacuuming the hall outside my room at 7:30 a.m.

(A) Don't worry—I'll talk to the concierge and make sure that doesn't happen this time.

(B) Don't worry—they're only cleaners.

(C) Don't worry—there are several good hotels in town that I can recommend.

III 你即將告辭，留你的客人愛德·莫里斯獨自在飯店。他曾提及，因為不懂中文，所以有點害怕一個人留在飯店。請利用下列詞語寫出一篇簡短的對話：

All the staff here speaks   if you need anything at all

the front desk   arrange for

＊解答請見 227 頁

第**3**章

介紹
Introductions

Introducing people is something we all have to do from time to time. If you're escorting a foreign guest around, it's something you'll be called upon to do all the more frequently.

介紹人是我們不時都需要做的事，如果你負責陪伴接送外國客人，一定會被要求更頻繁地做這件事。

1 Biz 必通句型 Need-to-Know Phrases

CD I-10

1.1 首次引見
Introducing People for the First Time

下列三句是基本介紹詞：

---

❶ (Person 1), I'd like you to meet (Person 2).（正式）
（某甲），容我介紹（某乙）給您認識。

例 Cameron McCash, I'd like you to meet Eugene Hung.
喀麥隆‧麥凱許，容我介紹尤京‧洪給您認識。

---

❷ (Person 1), I'd like to introduce (Person 2).（正式）
（某甲），容我向您介紹（某乙）。

例 Cameron McCash, I'd like to introduce Bruce Morton.
喀麥隆‧麥凱許，容我向您介紹布魯斯‧摩頓。

---

❸ (Person 1), this is (Person 2).（非正式）
（某甲），這位是（某乙）。

例 Cameron McCash, this is Chris.
喀麥隆‧麥凱許，這位是克里斯。

如果你想多介紹一下這個人的背景，下列這四句非常實用。

---

❹ (Person) is visiting us from (place).
（某人）是從（地方）來拜訪我們的。

例 Mr McCash is visiting us from Scotland.
麥凱許先生是從蘇格蘭來拜訪我們的。

---

❺ (Person) is with (company name).
（某人）在（公司名）服務。

例 Mr. McCash is with Highland Whiskeys.
麥凱許先生在高地威士忌公司服務。

❻ (Person) is in charge of (activity, <u>department</u>, etc.).
（某人）負責（單位、部門等）。

例 Eugene is in charge of our <u>litigation</u> department.
尤京負責我們的訴訟部門。

❼ (Person) <u>looks after</u> (activity, department, etc.) for us.
（某人）負責我們（單位、部門等）的業務。

例 Bruce looks after brand <u>enforcement</u> for us.
布魯斯負責我們品牌執行的業務。

介紹時稍微褒揚人幾句是好的。

❽ (Person) is one of our top....
（某人）是我們數一數二的……。

例 Eugene is one of our top litigators.
尤京是我們數一數二的訴訟律師。

Word List

department [dɪˋpɑrtmənt] *n.* 部門；局；處；科；系
litigation [ˏlɪtəˋgeʃən] *n.* 訴訟
look after [ˏlʊk ˋæftɚ] *phr. v.* 負責；照顧
enforcement [ɪnˋforsmənt] *n.* 實施；執行

1.2 再次介紹已見過面的人
Re-introducing People Who Have Already Met

❶ (Person 1), I believe you've already met (Person 2).
（正式）
（某甲），相信您已經見過（某乙）。
例 Anthony, I believe you've already met Dale.
安東尼，相信您已經見過戴爾。

❷ (Person 1), you (already) know (Person 2).（較不正式）
（某甲），你（已經）認識（某乙）。
例 Anthony, you already know Carla.
安東尼，你已經認識卡菈。

❸ Look who's back in town!（非正式，發自內心熱忱地說）
瞧瞧誰回來了！
例 Hey Jonathan, look who's back in town!
嘿，強納森，瞧瞧誰回來了！

❹ (Person 1), you remember (Person 2) from (place, event, etc.).（非正式）
（某甲），你記得（地方、事件等）的（某乙）吧。
例 Anthony, you remember Linda Hsieh from the <u>conference</u> in Seattle last year.
安東尼，你記得去年西雅圖會議上的琳達．謝吧。

Word **L**ist
conference [`kɑnfərəns] *n.* 針對某一主題持續數天的大型會議；協商會議

❺ **(Person 1), (I think) you know (Person 2) here, but I don't believe you've met (Person 3) yet.**（正式）
（某甲），（我想）您認識（某乙），但我相信您還沒見過（某丙）。
> 例 Anthony, I think you know Linda here, but I don't believe you've met Frances yet.
> 安東尼，我想您認識琳達，但我相信您還沒見過法蘭西斯。

❻ **I believe you (might) have already spoken to (Person) on the telephone.**
我相信您（可能）已經和（某人）通過電話了。
> 例 I believe you <u>might have</u> already <u>spoken</u> to Vivian on the telephone.
> 我相信您可能已經和薇薇安通過電話了。

❼ **(Person) is in town for (event, purpose, duration of stay, etc.)**
（某人）是為了（事件、目的、停留時間等）而來的。
> 例 Philip is in town for the <u>seminar</u> on brand protection.
> 菲力浦是為了參加品牌保護的研討會而來的。

❽ **<u>How rude of</u> me! I thought....**（當你忘記介紹某人時）
我真的太失禮了！我以為……。
> 例 How rude of me! I thought you two already knew each other.
> 我真的太失禮了！我以為你們兩位已經認識了。

Ⓦord List

might have done sth. 應該已經做了某事（might 為情態動詞，用來表示「假設、推論」）
seminar [ˈsɛməˌnɑr] *n.* 專題研討會
How adj. of sb.! 某人多麼地……！（如 How stupid of me! 我怎麼這麼笨呀！）

2 實戰會話 Show Time

2.1 Introducing People for the First Time

CD I-11

Three days later after the exposition, John and Terry have arrived in Taiwan. John has brought Terry to a <u>get-together</u> where several of John's <u>colleagues</u> are chatting over drinks. Terry has never been to Taiwan before.

John: Terry, I'd like you to meet Rex Liu. Rex is in charge of <u>Accounts</u> at Trenix.

Terry: Hi Rex. How are you?

Rex: Fine, thanks Terry. Welcome to Taiwan.

Terry: It's nice to be here.

John: And this is Aiko Tanaguchi. Aiko is one of our top designers.

Aiko: Hi Terry. It's very nice to meet you.

Terry: The pleasure is mine.

Aiko: How do you like Taiwan so far?

Terry: Well, I haven't seen very much of it yet, but I like what I've seen so far!

譯 文

首次引見

展覽會完三天後，約翰和泰瑞抵達台灣。約翰帶泰瑞去參加一場聚會，那裡有幾個約翰的同事在喝酒聊天。泰瑞之前從來沒來過台灣。

約翰：泰瑞，容我介紹雷克斯‧劉給您認識。雷克斯負責川尼斯的會計部門。

泰瑞：嗨！雷克斯，你好嗎？

雷克斯：還不錯，謝謝，泰瑞。歡迎來台灣。

泰瑞：很高興來這裡。

約翰：而這位是谷口愛子小姐。愛子是我們數一數二的設計師。

愛子：嗨！泰瑞，很高興認識你。

泰瑞：是我的榮幸。

愛子：目前為止您還喜歡台灣嗎？

泰瑞：這個嘛，我還沒去很多地方，但我喜歡目前為止看過的東西。

Word List

get-together [ˋgɛttəˏgɛðɚ] *n.* 非正式社交聚會
colleague [ˋkɑlig] *n.* 同事；同僚（亦可用 co-worker [ˋkoˏwɝkɚ] *n.*）
accounts [əˋkaʊnts] *n.*（複數形，不可數）財會部門

2.2 Re-introducing People Who Have Already Met

The next day John has brought Terry to meet some people from Trenix. Terry met some of the people in the group last year in London, but others he's meeting for the first time.

John: Everybody, there's someone I'd like you to meet. This is Terry—he's visiting the Trenix factory here in Taiwan.

Tanya: Look who's back in town! Well, I guess it was London where I saw you last, right?

Terry: Hi Tanya.

John: I totally forgot! You already know Tanya. And you remember James from the show in London last year, too?

Terry: Of course. How's it going, James? Nice to see you again.

James: Good to see you too, Terry.

John: Terry, this is Regina. I believe you might have already spoken to her on the telephone.

Terry: I did indeed. Hi Regina. It's nice to finally put a face to the name.

Regina: Hi Terry. Nice to meet you in person.

再次介紹已見過面的人

隔天約翰帶泰瑞去見川尼斯的一些人。泰瑞去年在倫敦見過其中幾位，但其他人則是第一次見面。

約翰：各位，有一個人我想介紹給大家認識。這位是泰瑞——他來台灣參觀川尼斯工廠。

譚雅：瞧瞧誰回來了！嗯，我想我上次看到你是在倫敦，對嗎？

泰瑞：嗨，譚雅。

約翰：我全忘了！您已經認識譚雅。您也還記得去年倫敦會展上的詹姆斯嗎？

泰瑞：當然。一切好嗎，詹姆斯？真高興再看到你。

詹姆斯：我也很高興再見到你，泰瑞。

約翰：泰瑞，這位是瑞婕娜。我相信您可能已經和她通過電話了。

泰瑞：我的確是。嗨！瑞婕娜，真高興終於看到妳的臉。

瑞婕娜：嗨，泰瑞，很高興看到你本人。

3 Biz 加分句型 Nice-to-Know Phrases

CD I-12

3.1 你和某人認識多久
How Long You've Known Someone

介紹時常會提及關係，下列這四句用來說明你和某人認識多久。

❶ **(Person) and I just met.**
我和（某人）剛認識。
例 Samantha and I just met.
我和莎曼珊剛認識。

❷ **(Person) and I have known each other since (time, event, etc.)**
（某人）和我從（時間、事件等）起就互相認識了。
例 Elaine and I have known each other since the summer of 2002.
伊蓮和我從2002年夏天起就互相認識了。

❸ **(Person) and I go way back.** （非正式，表示你和某人關係久遠）
（某人）和我早就認識了。
例 Cyrus and I go way back.
賽洛斯和我早就認識了。

❹ **(Person) and I have been working together since....**
（某人）和我從……就在一起工作了。
例 Gary and I have been working together since the company started in 1983.
蓋瑞和我從公司於1983年開創就在一起工作了。

3.2 再續前緣 Renewing Old <u>Acquaintances</u>

舊識重逢通常是件令人開心的事，不僅可以看到彼此的發展，應該也有
很多話題能夠聊。

❶ This visit will be a good chance for.... (介紹完舊識後用)
這次探訪是……的好機會。
例 This visit will be a good chance for you to get re-acquainted.
這次探訪是你們重新認識的好機會。

❷ I'll leave you alone to.... (引見後告辭時說)
我讓你們單獨……。
例 I'll leave you alone to get <u>caught-up</u>.
我讓你們單獨聚聚敘敘舊。

❸ This... will be a good chance for us to.... (對許久沒見的
舊識說)
這次……是我們……的好機會。
例 This <u>reunion</u> will be a good chance for us to get caught-up.
這次重聚是我們敘舊的好機會。

❹ It's been too long since....
自……已經太久了。
例 It's been too long since we've had a chance to talk.
距我們上次有機會聊天已經太久了。

Ⓦord List

acquaintance [ə`kwentəns] *n.* 相識的人
catch up [`kætʃ ˌʌp] *phr. v.* 聊天敘舊；趕上
reunion [ri`junjən] *n.* 重聚；再會合

4 Biz 加分字彙 Nice-to-Know Vocabulary

CD I-13

❶ **intern** [ˋɪntɝn] *n.* 實習生；實習教師；實習醫生

❷ **trainee** [treˋni] *n.* 受訓員；練習生

❸ **assistant** [əˋsɪstənt] *n.* 助理

❹ **specialist** [ˋspɛʃəlɪst] *n.* 專員

❺ **merchandise buyer** [ˋmɝtʃənˏdaɪz ˋbaɪɚ] *n.* 商品採購員

❻ **planner** [ˋplænɚ] *n.* 計劃人員；企劃

❼ **representative** [ˏrɛprɪˋzɛntətɪv] *n.* 代表

❽ **developer** [dɪˋvɛləpɚ] *n.* 開發人員；研發員

❾ **engineer** [ˏɛndʒəˋnɪr] *n.* 工程師

❿ **coordinator** [koˋɔrdnˏetɚ] *n.* 協調者

⓫ **supervisor** [ˏsupɚˋvaɪzɚ] *n.* 監督人員

⓬ **consultant** [kənˋsʌltənt] *n.* 顧問

⓭ **director** [dəˋrɛktɚ] *n.* 主管；總監；董事；導演

⓮ **vice president** [ˏvaɪs ˋprɛzədənt] *n.* 副總經理

⓯ **Chief Executive Officer** [ˋtʃif ɪgˋzɛkjʊtɪv ˋɔfəsɚ] *n.* (=CEO)

　　執行長

::::::::: 小心陷阱 :::::::::

☹ 錯誤用法

It's very nice to **see** you.

很高興認識你。

☺ 正確用法

It's very nice to **meet** you.

很高興認識你。

::::::::: 文化小叮嚀 :::::::::

In many foreign cultures, it is common to shake hands when saying hello or goodbye or when meeting someone for the first time. Some people <u>infer</u> a lot about a person from their hand-shake. A weak <u>grip</u> might be interpreted as a sign of a weak character—for this reason, avoid the "dead fish" handshake <u>at all costs</u>. Conversely, a grip that is too strong might come across as either <u>insecure</u> or overly <u>aggressive</u>—don't try to break anyone's bones. When shaking hands, aim for the <u>middle ground</u> with a firm and confident grip.

在很多外國文化中，見面問候、再見道別或首次相見時握手很普遍。有些人藉由握手的方式來推測許多事，握得有氣無力可能會被視為是個性軟弱的象徵——因此，無論如何都要避免「死魚式」的握手。相反地，握得太緊可能會被認為缺乏安全感或過分急進——所以千萬要注意別害人骨折。與人握手時，以力道適中為原則，要握得堅定而有自信。

ord List

infer [ɪnˋfɝ] v. 推論

grip [grɪp] n. 緊握

at all costs 無論如何

insecure [ˌɪnsɪˋkjʊr] adj. 不安全的

aggressive [əˋgrɛsɪv] adj. 侵略的；進取的

middle ground [ˋmɪdḷ ˋgraʊnd] n. 中間地帶

5 實戰演練 Practice Exercises

I 請為下列三題選出最適本章的中文譯義。

❶ from time to time

(A) 從以前到現在 (B) 間斷地 (C) 有時

❷ get-together

(A) 聯歡會 (B) 成果發表會 (C) 讀書研討會

❸ get caught-up

(A) 被逮捕 (B) 敘舊 (C) 被追上

II 你會如何回應下面這兩句話？

❶ I'll leave you alone to get caught-up.

(A) Why? Are we behind schedule again?

(B) OK, I'll talk to you later.

(C) Please don't leave us alone.

❷ Tonio and I go way back.

(A) Really? Where did you two meet?

(B) Back where?

(C) Really? I wish you weren't leaving so soon.

III 你要介紹你的客人，克提斯·梅，給你們公司的專利工程師，麥可·鄭。你和麥可是多年老友，而克提斯是為了電子商展而來的。請利用下列詞語寫出一篇簡短的對話：

I don't believe you've met	in town for	is one of our top
have known each other since	will be a good chance for us to	

＊解答請見 228 頁

第4章

咖啡店和茶館
Coffee Shops and Teahouses

Taking time out of a busy day for a relaxing cup of coffee or tea is one of the simple pleasures in life—for some, it is a ritual. It can mean ducking into a street-corner coffee shop on the spur-of-the-moment to grab a quick cup to go, or it can take the form of a pilgrimage to a mountain teahouse, where you can linger over steaming teacups, far from the noise and the city lights.

在忙碌的一天中抽空喝杯咖啡或茶紓解一下壓力是生活的簡趣之一——對某些人而言，這甚至是一項例行公事。你可能一時興起閃入街角的咖啡店抓一杯帶走，或以朝聖的方式到山上的茶館，捧著熱騰騰的茶杯慢慢品嚐，遠離喧囂和城市燈火。

1 Biz 必通句型 Need-to-Know Phrases

CD I-14

1.1 咖啡 Coffee

點餐時詢問客人的想法是種禮貌。

> ❶ **Do you want to have a... here, or get one to go?**
> 您想要在這裡喝杯……，還是帶一杯走？
> 例 Do you want to have a latté here, or get one to go?
> 您想要在這裡喝杯拿鐵，還是帶一杯走？

如果客人看不懂項目單板的話，你應該稍微解釋一下。

> ❷ **The coffee of the day is....**
> 本日咖啡是……。
> 例 The coffee of the day is Columbian.
> 本日咖啡是哥倫比亞咖啡。

下面四句告訴你如何形容咖啡的口味。

> ❸ **... is a (light/medium/dark) <u>roast</u>.**
> ……屬於（輕度／中度／深度）烘焙。
> 例 Kenyan coffee is a dark roast.
> 肯亞咖啡屬於深度烘焙。

> ❹ **... has a real <u>kick</u> to it.**
> ……的勁道十足。
> 例 Espresso coffee has a real kick to it.
> 義式濃縮咖啡的勁道十足。

Word List

roast [rost] *n.* 烘焙；烘烤

kick [kɪk] *n.* 興奮感或快感

❺ ... has a (<u>hearty</u>/<u>robust</u>/bitter etc.) <u>aroma</u>.

……的香味（濃厚／濃醇／苦等）。

例 Blue mountain coffee has a robust aroma.

藍山咖啡的香味濃醇。

❻ ... has a(n) (hearty/<u>full-bodied</u>/<u>aromatic</u>/<u>rich</u> etc.) flavor.

……的風味（濃厚／醇重／香醇／濃郁等）。

例 Kona coffee has a hearty flavor.

夏威夷火山可娜咖啡的風味濃厚。

通常店員會問你需要幾包糖和幾個奶油球。

❼ I take... creams and... sugars.

我要……個奶油球和……包糖。

例 I take two creams and one sugar.

我要兩個奶油球和一包糖。

❽ I don't take... in my coffee.

我的咖啡不加……。

例 I don't take sugar in my coffee.

我的咖啡不加糖。

Word List

hearty [ˈhɑrtɪ] *adj.*（食物）豐盛的；（人）熱忱的、有活力的

robust [rəˈbʌst] *adj.*（食物）豐富、濃醇的；（人）強健的

aroma [əˈromə] *n.* 香氣

full-bodied [fulˈbɑdɪd] *adj.*（飲料）口感醇重的；（事物）重要的

aromatic [ˌærəˈmætɪk] *adj.* 氣味香醇的

rich [rɪtʃ] *adj.*（食物）濃郁、油膩的；（色彩）濃艷的

1.2 茶 Tea

儘管紅茶是西方的傳統飲料，綠茶受歡迎的程度亦與日俱增，你可能還是比你的客人更熟悉中國茶和喝茶的規矩。

❶ ... is good to drink if you....
假如你……的話，喝……是好的。
例 Green tea is good to drink if you feel like your energy is low.
假如你覺得精神不濟的話，喝綠茶是好的。

❷ The tea should (only) be allowed to <u>steep</u> for (<u>duration</u>).
這種茶應該（只）可以泡（持續時間）。
例 The tea should be allowed to steep for another couple of minutes.
這種茶應該可以再多泡幾分鐘。

❸ ... should be prepared/served in (type of <u>tea ware</u>).
……應該要用（茶具種類）沖泡／上。
例 Oolong tea should be served in purple <u>clay</u> tea ware.
上烏龍茶應該要用紫砂茶具。

❹ This kind of tea grows well in..., like....
這種茶在……長得好，像……。
例 This kind of tea grows well in wet, cool climates, like the central mountains of Taiwan.
這種茶在像台灣中部山區這樣的濕冷氣候中長得好。

Ⓦord List

steep [stip] *v.* 浸泡
duration [dju`reʃən] *v.* 持續（存在）的時間；期間

tea ware [`ti ˌwɛr] *n.* 茶具
clay [kle] *n.* 黏土；泥土

很多外國人會有興趣進一步了解喝茶的文化和規矩。

❺ There are many customs <u>surrounding</u> tea drinking in Chinese culture.

中華文化中關於喝茶的習俗有很多。

例 There are many customs surrounding tea drinking in Chinese culture—one such custom is to only fill a guest's teacup <u>seven-tenths</u> full.

中華文化中關於喝茶的習俗有很多——其中之一就是只將客人的茶杯斟七分滿。

❻ There are numerous advantages to drinking tea.

喝茶的好處非常多。

例 There are numerous advantages to drinking tea—for instance, tea is rich in vitamins.

喝茶的好處非常多——比如，茶富含維生素。

❼ Every part of the Chinese tea ceremony is rich in symbolism.

中國茶藝的每一部分都富含象徵意義。

例 Every part of the Chinese tea ceremony is rich in symbolism—for example, serving tea can be a symbol of <u>togetherness</u>.

中國茶藝的每一部分都富含象徵意義——例如，奉茶能代表"團結"。

❽ For me, a cup of tea is best enjoyed while....

對我而言，在……時喝茶最好喝。

例 For me, a cup of tea is best enjoyed while soaking in a hot bath.

對我而言，在泡熱水澡時喝茶最好喝。

ord List

surround [sə`raʊnd] v. 與……相關；環繞

seven-tenths [`sɛvṇˌtɛnθs] n. 十分之七（分數 fraction 的英文書寫方式為：分子用英文基數 [one, ten, twenty-one...] 表示，分母用英文序數 [first, tenth, twenty-first...] 表示；如分子大於1，分母的英文序數需加 s，如：1/8 為 one-eighth，2/3 為 two-thirds）

togetherness [tə`gɛðə·nɪs] n. 團結；親密與共

2 實戰會話 Show Time

2.1 The Coffee Shop

John and Terry are <u>walking down</u> the street early in the morning. As they pass a coffee shop, a cup of coffee seems like a good idea.

Terry: I really need to wake up before the meeting....

John: You're in luck—here's a coffee shop. Do you want to have a coffee here, or get one to go?

Terry: Let's get them to go. We don't have too much time.

John: The menu board says the coffee of the day is French breakfast roast. How does that sound to you?

Terry: Yeah, that works.

John: How do you take your coffee?

Terry: I take double cream.

John: No sugar?

Terry: No, I don't take sugar in my coffee.

咖啡店

約翰和泰瑞一早走在街上。當他們經過一家咖啡店時，來杯咖啡似乎是個好主意。

泰瑞：開會之前我實在需要好好清醒……。

約翰：您的運氣不錯——這裡有家咖啡店。您想要在這裡喝，還是帶走？

泰瑞：外帶好了，我們沒有太多時間。

約翰：價目單版上寫著：本日咖啡是法式烘焙早餐咖啡。您覺得如何？

泰瑞：好啊，就是它了。

約翰：您的咖啡要怎麼喝？

泰瑞：我要雙倍奶油。

約翰：不要糖嗎？

泰瑞：不要，我喝咖啡不加糖。

 ord List

walk down 沿著……走

2.2 The Teahouse

It's later in the day and Terry and John have headed out beyond the <u>outskirts</u> of the city for a <u>leisurely</u> cup of tea in a typical Chinese-style teahouse.

Terry: I've never been to a real teahouse before. What a great <u>atmosphere</u>!

John: It's very <u>relaxing</u>, isn't it? For me, a cup of tea is always best enjoyed on a mountainside like this, looking out at the view.

Terry: So what kind of tea are we going to drink?

John: It's Oolong. Oolong tea is good to drink if you want to lose weight or <u>build up</u> your body.

Terry: Well, I'<u>m</u> not really <u>looking to</u> do either, but that's OK....

John: It's delicious, most of all. This kind of tea grows well in <u>subtropical</u> climates, like Taiwan.

Terry: Everything seems so <u>ritualized</u>....

John: It is. Every part of the Chinese tea ceremony is rich in symbolism—for example, my pouring tea for you is my way of showing my <u>esteem</u> for an honored guest.

譯文

茶館

當天稍晚，泰瑞和約翰前往市郊外一家典型的中式茶館悠閒地喝茶。

泰瑞：我以前從來沒到過真正的茶館。這裡氣氛真棒！

約翰：很輕鬆，不是嗎？對我而言，在像這樣的山邊往外看著風景喝茶最好喝
了。

泰瑞：那，我們要喝哪種茶？

約翰：烏龍。如果您想減肥或健身的話，喝烏龍茶是好的。

泰瑞：嗯，我沒有這兩項計劃，不過沒關係……。

約翰：最重要的是，它很好喝。這種茶在像台灣這樣的亞熱帶氣候中長得好。

泰瑞：一切似乎都要照規矩走……。

約翰：的確是。中國茶藝的每一部分都富含象徵意義──例如，我幫您倒茶就
是我表達對貴賓尊敬的方式。

Ｗord List

outskirts [`aʊt͵skɝts] *n.* （複數形）郊區；城市外圍
leisurely [`liʒɚlɪ] *adj.* 悠閒的；*adv.* 從容不迫地
atmosphere [`ætməs͵fɪr] *n.* 氣氛；空氣
relaxing [rɪ`læksɪŋ] *adj.* 令人放鬆的
build up [͵bɪld `ʌp] *phr. v.* 使增大；增進
be looking to do sth. 計劃做某事
subtropical [sʌb`trɑpɪkḷ] *adj.* 亞熱帶的
ritualized [`rɪtʃʊəl͵aɪzd] *adj.* 儀式化的
esteem [ɪs`tim] *n.* 尊重；尊敬

3 Biz 加分句型 Nice-to-Know Phrases

3.1 點對東西 Getting the Order Right

點東西是門學問，使用下列這四句幫你自己和客人點出想要的東西。

❶ Do you want a...?
你要一杯……？
例 Do you want a small, a medium, or a large?
你想要小杯、中杯還是大杯？

❷ How do you take your...?
你要怎麼喝你的……？
例 How do you take your tea?
你的茶要怎麼喝？

❸ What do you take in your...?
你的……要加什麼？
例 What do you take in your coffee?
你的咖啡要加什麼？

❹ Do you need...?
你需要……嗎？
例 Do you need sugar or cream?
你需要糖或奶油嗎？

1.2 咖啡或茶的產地 The Origins of a Coffee or Tea

台灣名茶的產區主要分布在嘉義縣、南投縣、台中縣等地，此區茶葉數量為全台最大，品質與品種皆非常穩定且與日精進。

❶ This coffee/tea is grown....

這種茶／咖啡產於……。

例 This coffee is grown locally—it comes from Cukeng.

這種咖啡是本地出產的——它來自古坑。

❷ This coffee/tea is imported from....

這種咖啡／茶是從……進口的。

例 This Darjeeling tea is imported from India.

這種大吉嶺紅茶是從印度進口的。

❸ This coffee/tea is exported to....

這種咖啡／茶外銷到……。

例 This Ti Kuan Yin is exported to Europe.

這種鐵觀音外銷到歐洲。

❹ This... is a coffee/tea from..., it has a.... flavor.

這種……是產自……的一種咖啡／茶，它有一種……風味。

例 This Assam tea is a tea from northern India, it has a malty flavor.

這種阿薩姆紅茶是產自印度北部的一種茶，它有種麥芽味。

Ⓦord List

Darjeeling [dɑr`ʤilɪŋ] *n.* 大吉嶺紅茶；印度北部的大吉嶺地區

Assam [æ`sæm] *n.* 阿薩姆（印度東北部的一省）

malty [`mɔltɪ] *adj.* 麥芽的

4 Biz 加分字彙 Nice-to-Know Vocabulary

CD I-17

❶ mocha [`mokə] *n.* 摩卡

❷ cappuccino [ˌkɑpə`tʃino] *n.* 卡布奇諾

❸ caramel macchiato [`kærəml̩ mɑki`ɑto] *n.* 焦糖瑪琪朵

❹ blend [blɛnd] *n.* 混合物；混合

❺ syrup [`sɪrəp] *n.* 糖漿；醫藥糖漿

❻ decaffeinated [di`kæfiˌnetɪd] *adj.* 低咖啡因的；脫除咖啡因的

❼ white tea [`hwaɪt `ti] *n.* 白茶

❽ flower tea [`flauɚ `ti] *n.* 花茶

❾ herbal tea [`hɝbl̩ `ti] *n.* 草本茶；花草茶

❿ organic tea [ɔr`gænɪk `ti] *n.* 有機茶

⓫ compressed tea [kəm`prɛst `ti] *n.* 緊壓茶；壓縮茶

⓬ jasmine tea [`dʒæsmɪn `ti] *n.* 茉莉綠茶（俗稱香片，屬花茶）

⓭ white peony tea [`hwaɪt `piənɪ `ti] *n.* 白牡丹茶（屬白茶）

⓮ Long Jing 龍井（屬綠茶）

⓯ Pu Erh 普洱茶（屬黑茶）

小心陷阱

☹ 錯誤用法
I **eat** my coffee black.
我喝黑咖啡。

☺ 正確用法
I **take** my coffee black.
我喝黑咖啡。

文化小叮嚀

Many people like to have a cup of coffee to wake up in the morning. If you're having an early start, showing up with a cup of coffee for your guest is a <u>courtesy</u> that can earn you some <u>brownie points</u>. It's a little thing, but don't overlook the importance of such small gestures when building a business relationship—they add up!

In Western restaurants, it is common to serve coffee after both lunch and dinner meals. In some Western countries, it is common to add things like sugar, milk, and honey to tea. When serving guests Chinese tea, you can assure them that such <u>additions</u> would only <u>detract</u> from the taste of the beverage.

很多人喜歡早上喝杯咖啡來醒腦。假如你們一早就有行程，現身時為客人帶杯咖啡這樣貼心的禮貌可以幫你贏得許多分數。這雖然只是件小事，但在培養商業關係時，千萬別忽略這種小舉動的重要性——它們會逐漸累積！

在西式餐廳，用完午餐和晚餐後上咖啡相當普通。在某些西方國家中，通常都會在茶裡面加糖、牛奶和蜂蜜調味；請客人喝中國茶時，你可以明確地告訴他們加這些東西只會破壞茗品的風味。

Word List

courtesy[ˋkɝtəsɪ] *n.* 禮貌；*adj.* 免費提供的（如機場常見 courtesy phone，即為服務旅客設的免費電話）

brownie points [ˋbraʊnɪ ˌpɔɪnts] *n.* （通常複數）記優點；加分（由女童軍 brownie 獎賞制度而來）

addition [əˋdɪʃən] *n.* 增加的人或物；加法

detract [dɪˋtrækt] *v.* 減損；損害

5 實戰演練 Practice Exercises

I 請為下列兩題選出最適本章的中文譯義。

❶ have a real kick

(A)十分受歡迎　(B)勁道十足　(C)非常刺激

❷ build up

(A)開發　(B)增強　(C)誇大

II 你會如何回答下面這兩句話？

❶ What do you take in your coffee?

(A) I take it to work in the morning.

(B) I take it black—no cream or sugar.

(C) I take it in a cup, doesn't everyone?

❷ Where does this coffee come from?

(A) This coffee is exported all over the world.

(B) From that big coffee pot behind the counter.

(C) This coffee is imported from Brazil.

III 你的客人問你本日咖啡是哪一種，回答他們，並解說一下這種咖啡
的特色（咖啡特色經常會標示出來讓顧客參考）。請利用下列詞語寫
出一篇簡答：

coffee of the day	roast	aroma
flavor	give it a try	

＊解答請見 229 頁

第 **5** 章

正式晚宴／宴會
Formal Dinner/Banquet

Often, visiting guests will be invited to attend a formal company dinner or banquet. These special events can make a big impression on your guest and can help to foster good business relationships. The way to a client's heart just might be through their stomach!

訪客時常會被邀請參加公司的正式晚宴或宴會，這些特別的場合能使客人留下深刻的印象，並且有助於增進良好的商業關係。要抓住客戶的心，可能需要先滿足他們的胃！

1 Biz 必通句型 Need-to-Know Phrases

CD I-18

1.1 告知客人晚宴／宴會
Informing a Guest About the Dinner/Banquet

下列這三句話用來通知客人即將舉行的宴會。

❶ ... has/have arranged a banquet (date/time) for (attendees) at (place).

……已經安排好（日期／時間）在（地方）設筵款待（出席人員）。

例 Mr. Kwan, the president, has arranged a banquet tomorrow night for the conference delegates at a nice restaurant downtown.

總裁關先生已經安排好明晚在市區一家高級餐廳設筵款待會議代表。

❷ (Attendees) are invited to attend.

敬邀（出席人員）光臨。

例 All the Asian Regional Managers are invited to attend.

敬邀所有亞洲區經理光臨。

❸ Dinner will be served at (time).

晚宴將在（時間）開席。

例 Dinner will be served at seven o'clock.

晚宴將在七點開席。

抵達宴會地點後，下列這三句話能幫助客人適應環境。

Ｗord List

attendee [ə`tɛndi] *n.* 出席者
delegate [`dɛləgɪt] *n.* 代表 (=representative)；*v.* [`dɛlə‚get] 指派
attend [ə`tɛnd] *v.* 出席；參加

❹ You're sitting (location), next to (person A) and (person B).

您坐（位置），隔壁是（某甲）和（某乙）。

例 You're sitting here, next to Jerry Lin and Loretta Kim.

您坐這裡，隔壁是傑瑞·林和羅莉塔·金。

❺ Following dinner there will be....

晚宴後會有……。

例 Following dinner there will be live entertainment.

晚宴後還有現場表演。

❻ Dinner will be a (number)-course meal of (type of <u>cuisine</u>) food.

晚宴將是（道數）道的（料理種類）菜。

例 Dinner will be a twelve-course meal of Szechuan Chinese food.

晚宴會是 12 道的中式川菜。

宴會經常都會安排致詞，不妨讓客人知道致詞者將會是誰。

❼ ... is scheduled to give a speech (before/after/during)....

……預定於……（前／後／時）致詞。

例 Paul Beam is scheduled to give a speech after the meal.

保羅·畢姆預定於用餐後致詞。

❽ ... is the <u>keynote</u> speaker.

……是主要的致詞貴賓。

例 Mary Beam is the keynote speaker.

瑪莉·畢姆是主要的致詞貴賓。

Ⓦord List

cuisine [kwɪˋzin] *n.* 特定的烹調方式；料理；菜餚

keynote [ˋkiˌnot] *n.* 主旨；基調

1.2 席上 At the Table

用餐時問一下客人是否喜歡菜餚湯飲是非常體貼的舉動。

❶ ... is delicious, isn't it?

……很好吃，不是嗎？

例 The <u>grilled</u> sea <u>bass</u> is delicious, isn't it?

這道燒烤鱸魚很好吃，不是嗎？

❷ Will you have some more of...?

您要不要再來一點……？

例 Will you have some more of the <u>stuffed tomatoes</u>?

您要不要再來一點鑲番茄？

❸ Have you tried the (<u>dish</u>)?

您試過（菜）了嗎？

例 Have you tried the fried <u>eel</u>?

您試過炸鰻魚了嗎？

若客人之前從未來過你的國家，可能要稍微解說一下本地料理特色。

❹ ... cuisine is known for being (adj.).

……菜以……出名。

例 Shanghainese cuisine is known for being heavy and rather oily.

上海菜以口味重而且很油膩出名。

Ⓦord List

grill [grɪld] *adj.* 烤的

bass [`bæs] *n.* 鱸魚；鱸魚肉

stuffed tomato [`stʌft tə`meto] *n.* 鑲番茄
（將番茄肉挖出，以番茄為盅填入鮪魚等肉
類及香辛料）

dish [dɪʃ] *n.* 一盤菜；菜餚；盤子

eel [il] *n.* 鰻魚；鰻魚肉

❺ ... is/are the (<u>appetizer</u>/<u>starter</u>/<u>hors d'oeuvre</u>).

......是開胃菜。

例 Corn soup is the appetizer.

玉米湯是開胃前菜。

❻ ... is the (<u>main course</u>/<u>entrée</u>).

......是主菜。

例 Lemon Chicken is the main course.

檸檬雞是主菜。

❼ You can add (sauce/spice) to the (dish) to give it more flavor.

您可以加點（醬料／辛香調味料）到（菜）以增加風味。

例 You can add <u>gravy</u> to the pork to give it more flavor.

您可以淋點肉汁到豬肉上以增加風味。

❽ For dessert we're having....

我們的甜點是……。

例 For dessert we're having Baked Alaska.

我們的甜點是「火焰雪山」。

ord List

appetizer [ˋæpəˏtaɪzɚ] *n.* 開胃菜

starter [ˋstɑrtɚ] *n.* 開胃菜；第一道菜

hors d'oeuvre [ˋɔrˏdɜv] *n.* 開胃菜

main course [ˋmen ˋkors] *n.* 主菜

entrée [ˋɑntre] *n.* （美）主菜

gravy [ˋgrevɪ] *n.* 肉汁

2 實戰會話 Show Time

CD I-19

2.1 A Company Dinner

The company president has arranged a formal dinner at an elegant hotel to welcome Terry to Taiwan. John is telling Terry what to <u>expect</u>.

John: Mr. Huang, the president, has arranged a banquet tonight for the company <u>brass</u> at a hotel near your hotel. You're the guest of honor!

Terry: I'm flattered. What time is the banquet?

John: Dinner will be served at six-thirty. Following dinner there will be a couple of speeches. It shouldn't run too late.

Terry: I'll make sure I have a few words prepared myself. What's on the menu?

John: I don't know exactly. What I do know is that dinner will be a <u>multi</u>-course meal of Szechuan style Chinese food. It's the boss's favorite.

Terry: What kind of food is that?

John: Szechuan is a <u>province</u> in the western part of China, and the food there is known for being hot and spicy, as well as delicious!

Terry: Gee, I can't wait. I'll bring my <u>appetite</u>!

公司晚宴

公司總裁在一家精緻的酒店安排了一場正式晚宴歡迎泰瑞到台灣來，約翰正在向和泰瑞解說可能的場景。

約翰：總裁黃先生，已經安排好今晚在您下榻飯店附近的一家酒店設筵款待公司的主管人員，而您是榮譽貴賓！

泰瑞：真不敢當。宴會在什麼時候開始？

約翰：晚宴將在六點半開席。晚宴後會有幾場致詞，但應該不會到太晚。

泰瑞：我一定會自己先準備幾句話。菜色有哪些？

約翰：我不太清楚，但我知道晚宴會是多道的中式川菜，那是老闆的最愛。

泰瑞：那是什麼樣的食物？

約翰：四川是中國西部的一個省份，那裡的食物以辛辣出名，還有美味！

泰瑞：哇，我等不及了。我會把胃口帶去！

Word List

expect [ɪk`spɛkt] *v.* 預期；期盼
brass [bræs] *n.* 銅；銅製品；高階軍官；企業高級主管
multi-[`mʌltɪ]（字首）多重、複合的（與名詞或形容詞連用，如 multimedia *n./adj.* 多媒體（的）、multilingual *adj.* 使用多種語言的）
province [`prɑvɪns] *n.* 省
appetite [`æpə͵taɪt] *n.* 食慾；胃口；慾望

2.2 At the Table

Terry and John are sitting at the head table at the banquet. The table is covered in delicious food. Mr. Huang, the company president, wants to make sure his American guest is getting enough to eat.

Mr. Huang: How is the food, Mr. Matthews?

Terry: Everything is just excellent, thanks....

Mr. Huang: The <u>peppered</u> beef is delicious, isn't it?

Terry: <u>Absolutely</u> wonderful, although I like the Kung Pao Chicken even better!

Mr. Huang: Have you had Szechuan food before?

Terry: I've had some of these dishes before back in the hometown where I live, but it was nothing like this —I feel like I'm in food heaven!

Mr. Huang: Will you have some more of the <u>spinach</u>?

Terry: Thanks, don't mind if I do.... (*Helping himself.*)

Mr. Huang: Szechuan cuisine is known for being spicy. I hope it's not too hot for your taste....

Terry: Not at all—I like it hot!

 譯文

席上

宴會中泰瑞和約翰坐在主桌，桌上擺滿了美食。公司總裁黃先生，想確定他的美國客人吃得盡興。

黃先生：菜還可以嗎，馬修士先生？

泰瑞：每一道菜都很棒，謝謝⋯⋯。

黃先生：這道胡椒牛肉很好吃，不是嗎？

泰瑞：的確非常美味，雖然我更喜歡宮保雞丁！

黃先生：您之前曾吃過四川菜嗎？

泰瑞：我以前在我住的老家曾吃過這些菜其中幾樣，但都不像這樣——我覺得我在美食天堂！

黃先生：您要不要再來一點菠菜？

泰瑞：謝謝，別介意我再吃一些⋯⋯。（*自取*）

黃先生：川菜以辣出名，希望您不會覺得太辣不對您的口味⋯⋯。

泰瑞：完全不會——我就是喜歡辣！

ord List

peppered [`pɛpəd] *adj.* 加了胡椒調味的
absolutely [`æbsə,lutlɪ] *adv.* 絕對地；完全地
spinach [`spɪnɪtʃ] *n.* （不可數）菠菜

3 Biz 加分句型 Nice-to-Know Phrases

 CD I-20

3.1 Offering Wine 倒酒

❶ Can I <u>top up</u> your (glass/drink)?
我把你的（杯子／飲料）斟滿好嗎？
例 Can I top up your wineglass?
我把你的酒杯斟滿好嗎？

❷ Would you care for some (drink/food)?
您想來點（飲料／食物）嗎？
例 Would you care for more wine?
您想再來點酒嗎？

❸ More wine,...?
要再來點酒嗎，……？
例 More wine, Mr. Ensor?
要再來點酒嗎，安索先生？

❹ How about some more...?
再來一些……怎樣？
例 How about some more beer, Mike?
邁克，再來一些啤酒怎樣？

 Word **L**ist

top up [ˌtɑp `ʌp] *phr. v.* 將……盛滿

3.2 鼓勵客人吃菜 Encouraging Your Guest to Eat

用下面這句話來邀請客人／大家開動，並使場面輕鬆、熱絡。

❶ Don't wait—<u>dig in</u>!
等什麼——開動吧！

下列這三句話用來鼓勵客人多吃一點。

❷ Please,....
請……。
例 Please, help yourself.
請自己來。

❸ Let's not....
咱們別……。
例 Let's not let this food go to waste.
咱們別把這些菜給浪費掉了。

❹ Don't be shy about....
不要害羞……。
例 Don't be shy about having <u>seconds</u>.
別不好意思來第二盤。

ord List

dig in [ˌdɪg `ɪn] *phr. v.* 大口吃；開動（用來邀請別人進食並且盡可能多吃一些）
seconds [`sɛkəndz] *n.* （複數形）（食物的）第二份

4 Biz 加分字彙 Nice-to-Know Vocabulary

 CD I-21

① invitation [ˌɪnvəˈteʃən] *n.* 邀請；請帖

② dining etiquette [ˈdaɪnɪŋ ˈɛtɪkɛt] *n.* 用餐禮儀

③ table manners [ˈtebḷ ˈmænɚz] *n.* (複數形) 餐桌禮儀

④ table setting [ˈtebḷ ˈsɛtɪŋ] *n.* 餐桌擺設；排餐具

⑤ server [ˈsɝvɚ] *n.* 侍者；上菜者

⑥ host [ˈhost] *n.* 主人，hostess [ˈhostɪs] *n.* 女主人

⑦ napkin [ˈnæpkɪn] *n.* 餐巾；紙巾

⑧ saucer [ˈsɔsɚ] *n.* 小碟子；茶托

⑨ platter [ˈplætɚ] *n.* 大淺盤（通常為橢圓形）

⑩ stainless flatware [ˈstenlɪs ˈflætˌwɛr] *n.* 不銹鋼扁平餐具
（刀、叉、湯匙等）

⑪ salt shaker [ˈsɔlt ˈʃekɚ] *n.* 鹽巴罐

⑫ soy sauce [ˈsɔɪ ˌsɔs] *n.* 醬油

⑬ vinegar [ˈvɪnɪgɚ] *n.* 醋

⑭ dental floss [ˈdɛntḷ ˌflɔs] *n.* 牙線

⑮ doggy bag [ˈdɔgɪ ˌbæg] *n.* 用來打包的袋子或盒子

------- 小心陷阱 -------

☹ 錯誤用法

These speeches following dinner can sometimes be **bored**.

晚宴後的致詞有時候會很無聊。

☺ 正確用法

These speeches following dinner can sometimes be **boring**.

晚宴後的致詞有時候會很無聊。

------- 文化小叮嚀 -------

If Westerners are coming to dinner, they may or may not be <u>adept</u> at using chopsticks. As a courtesy, make sure that the restaurant has clean silverware (knives and forks) <u>on hand</u> for your foreign guests to use. Similarly, ensure that there are serving chopsticks for each dish—some foreigners might be uncomfortable with the practice of <u>communal</u> eating where everyone helps themselves from a dish using their own chopsticks.

If your guest does not speak the local language, try to make sure he or she is seated beside people who speak English whenever possible so they won't feel too <u>isolated</u>.

Some Westerners do not enjoy eating <u>organ</u> meats. Don't be <u>offended</u> by their <u>refusal</u> to try these dishes. Just remember, this kind of food might not be part of your guest's culture.

假如有西方人要來參加晚宴，他們不一定都很會使用筷子，為了禮貌起見，應確定餐廳備有乾淨的銀器（刀子和叉子）可供外國客人使用。同樣地，還需確定每道菜都擺了公筷——有些外國人對於每個人用私筷從菜盤中自助取食這樣的共食習慣也許不太舒服。

如果你的客人不會講本地語言，盡可能安排他／她坐在會講英語的人的旁邊，這樣他們才不會覺得過於孤立。有些西方人不喜歡吃內臟，如果他們拒絕嘗試，不要覺得受到冒犯。要記得，這種食物或許不是你客人文化的一部分。

Word List

adept [əˋdɛpt] *adj.* 熟練的（be ~ at N./V-ing 對……很在行、拿手）

on hand 在手邊或近處可供使用

communal [ˋkɑmjʊnḷ] *adj.* 共有的；社區的

isolated [ˋaɪsḷˌetɪd] *adj.* 孤立的；隔離的

organ [ˋɔrgən] *n.* 器官；管風琴

offend [əˋfɛnd] *v.* 冒犯；觸怒

refusal [rɪˋfjuzḷ] *n.* 拒絕

5 實戰演練 Practice Exercises

I 請為下列三題選出最適本章的中文譯義。

❶ company brass

(A) 公司高級主管 (B) 連隊高階軍官 (C) 劇團銅管樂器

❷ care for...

(A) 在乎…… (B) 照顧…… (C) 想要……

❸ dig in

(A) 埋入 (B) 奮鬥 (C) 開動

II 你會如何回應下面這兩句話？

❶ Can I top up your wineglass?

(A) I'd prefer it if you drank your own.

(B) I don't think it will hold your weight.

(C) I'll have a little more, thanks.

❷ You'll be sitting at the head table.

(A) I've never eaten head before.

(B) I'm honored.

(C) I have to put my head where?

III 你是一家大型汽車公司的主管，正在向客人解說餐廳的菜單，你們將和其他公司的主管一起用餐。請利用下列詞語寫出一篇簡短的解說：

banquet	course meal	Sri Lankan	cuisine
appetizer	main course	dessert	

＊解答請見 230 頁

第 **6** 章

參觀工廠
A Tour of the Plant

A tour of the office, factory, call center, warehouse, or assembly plant often makes up part of a visiting guest's itinerary. It's a chance for them to have a look at what they're buying into, as well as a chance for you to show off your company's facilities.

一趟辦公室、工廠、客服中心、倉庫或組裝廠的參觀行程經常構成訪客預定行程的一部分，這是他們看看自己做的選擇的機會，也是你展示公司設備的良機。

1 Biz 必通句型 Need-to-Know Phrases

 CD I-22

1.1 討論公司 Discussing the Company

一般都會從最基本的資料開始——公司什麼時候成立及營運業務等。

❶ ... was founded in (year) by....
……於（年份）由……所創立。
例 Celebron was founded in 1992 by Mr. Yeung, the President and CEO.
賽勒布隆於 1992 年由總裁兼執行長楊先生所創立。

❷ ... is a leading... of....
……是一家……的領導……。
例 Workhorse is a leading supplier of <u>packaging</u> and shipping <u>materials</u>.
役馬是一家包裝與物料運送的領導供應商。

❸ This is the (type of <u>facility</u> name) where we....
這是我們……的（設備種類名稱）。
例 This is the plant where we <u>assemble</u> the <u>chipsets</u>.
這是我們裝配晶片組的工廠。

參觀設備時，一定要適時地展現公司的強項。

❹ As you can see, the... is <u>state-of-the-art</u>.
如您所見，……非常先進。
例 As you can see, the <u>laboratory</u> is state-of-the-art.
如您所見，實驗室非常先進。

Word List

packaging [`pækɪdʒɪŋ] *n.* 包裝作業；盒、封面等包裝物
material [mə`tɪrɪəl] *n.* 原料；材料；布料
facility [fə`sɪlətɪ] *n.* 設備；工具；場所

assemble [ə`sɛmbl] *v.* 配裝；組合
chipset [`tʃɪp͵sɛt] *n.* 晶片組
state-of-the-art [`stetəvði `ɑrt] *adj.* 先進的
laboratory [`læbrə͵torɪ] *n.* (=lab) 實驗室

❺ Our... <u>incorporates</u> <u>cutting-edge</u> technology to produce... of the highest quality.

我們的……融合尖端科技來生產最高品質的……。

例 Our production facility incorporates cutting-edge technology to produce <u>capacitors</u> and <u>insulators</u> of the highest quality.

我們的生產設備融合尖端科技來生產最高品質的電容器和絕緣器。

❻ <u>Stringent</u> quality controls <u>are in place to</u> ensure....

實施嚴格的品管以確保……。

例 As you can see, stringent quality controls are in place to ensure that all units meet or <u>exceed</u> the required industry <u>specifications</u>.

如您所見，我們執行嚴格的品管以確保所有的組件都能符合或超越業界要求的規格。

❼ (Doing/Not doing)... helps us keep costs down.

（做／不做）……幫助我們減低成本。

例 Using local materials helps us keep costs down.

使用當地原料幫助我們減低成本。

❽ ... employs a total <u>workforce</u> of (number of workers).

……雇用的員工總人數有（員工數量）。

例 Celebron employs a total workforce of two hundred and fifty workers.

賽勒布隆雇用的員工總人數達 250 位。

Ｗord List

incorporate [ɪnˋkɔrpəˌret] *v.* 加入；融合

cutting-edge [ˋkʌtɪŋ ˋɛdʒ] *adj.* 尖端的

capacitor [kəˋpæsətɚ] *n.* 電容器

insulator [ˋɪnsəˌletɚ] *n.* 絕緣器；絕緣體

stringent [ˋstrɪndʒənt] *adj.* 嚴格的

be in place to... 存在以……

exceed [ɪkˋsid] *v.* 超過；超越

specification [ˌspɛsəfəˋkeʃən] *n.* 規格；詳細計劃書

workforce [ˋwɚkˌfors] *n.* 員工數；勞動力

1.2 談論相關業務 Talking Shop

下列四句能讓客人對你們公司的運作有初步的認識。

❶ Our... produces... units every (time period).

我們的……每（時期）生產……個組件。

例 Our Wugu factory produces 700 units every day.

我們的五股工廠每天生產 700 個組件。

❷ We use the most up-to-date....

我們採用最新的……。

例 We use the most up-to-date management techniques.

我們採用最新的管理技術。

❸ We've imported a lot of... and incorporated them into....

我們引進許多的……，並將它們融入……。

例 We've imported a lot of foreign management philosophies and incorporated them into our production process.

我們引進許多國外的管理觀念，並將它們融入我們的生產流程。

❹ Having... located... allows us to....

有……位在……，使得我們可以……。

例 Having our warehouse located close to the port allows us to transport our products cheaply and easily.

我們的倉庫臨近港口，使得我們可以便宜、輕易地運送我們的產品。

ord List

up-to-date [`ʌptə `det] *adj.* 最新的
management [`mænɪdʒmənt] *n.* 管理
philosophy [fə`lɑsəfɪ] *n.* 哲學；原理

process [`prɑsɛs] *n.* 程序；過程；製作法
warehouse [`wɛr,haʊs] *n.* 倉庫
transport [træns`pɔrt] *v.* 運送

當然，你應該會想強調公司產品具有特色的原因。

❺ At..., we insist on using only the....
在……，我們堅持只用……。
例 At CookieWorks, we insist on using only the freshest <u>ingredients</u>.
在餅乾工坊，我們堅持只用最新鮮的原料。

❻ The... was <u>renovated</u>/modernized (time period).
……（時期）被翻修／更新過。
例 The <u>workshop</u> was renovated last January.
這座工坊去年一月翻修過。

下列這句話在引導客人移動腳步時非常好用。

❼ If you've seen enough here, let's take a look at ... next.
假如這裡您已經看得差不多了，接下來我們去看……。
例 If you've seen enough here, let's take a look at the <u>call center</u> next.
如果這裡您已經看得差不多了，我們接下來去看看客服中心。

❽ That pretty much <u>concludes</u> our tour,.... I hope you've enjoyed it.
我們的行程到這裡差不多結束 ，……。希望這趟參觀您還滿意。
例 That pretty much concludes our tour, Mr. Reed. I hope you've enjoyed it.
我們的行程到這裡差不多結束，瑞德先生。希望這趟參觀您還滿意。

 Word List

ingredient [ɪnˋɡridɪənt] *n.* 原料；要素
renovate [ˋrɛnəˌvet] *v.* 翻修；更新
workshop [ˋwɝkˌʃɑp] *n.* 工坊；研討會

call center （電話）客服中心（公司機構接應顧客來電及做電話行銷拜訪的作業單位，業務亦常包括電子郵件、傳真及書信等）
conclude [kənˋklud] *v.* 結束；做結論

2 實戰會話 Show Time

CD I-23

2.1 Introducing the Company

John has just had Terry <u>sign into</u> the Trenix plant where they assemble computer chipsets. He's showing Terry around and telling him about the <u>nuts and bolts</u> of the <u>operation</u>.

John: This is the facility where we assemble the <u>flat-screen monitors</u>. As you can see, the tools we use are state-of-the-art.

Terry: And what are they doing over there? <u>Inspecting</u> <u>finished</u> units?

John: Exactly. Stringent quality controls are in place to ensure that we only <u>ship</u> the highest quality products.

Terry: It looks like a very <u>efficient</u> operation.

John: We like to think so. Our assembly plant produces 150 units a day.

介紹公司

約翰剛請泰瑞簽名進入川尼斯工廠，他們裝配電腦晶片組的地方。他帶泰瑞四處參觀，並向他解說業務運作的基本要項。

約翰：這是我們裝配平面監視器的設備。如您所見，我們使用的工具非常先進。

泰瑞：他們在那裡做什麼？檢驗成品嗎？

約翰：完全正確。我們執行嚴格的品管以確保我們只送出最高品質的產品。

泰瑞：作業看起來很有效率。

約翰：我們希望是。我們的裝配廠每天生產 150 個組件。

Word List

sign into [`saɪn ˌɪntu] *v.* 簽名進入

nuts and bolts [`nʌtsən `bolts] *n.* 基本細節

operation [ˌɑpə`reʃən] *n.* 營運；操作；手術

flat-screen [`flæt ˌskrin] *adj.* 平面螢幕的

monitor [`mɑnətɚ] *n.* 監視器

inspect [ɪn`spɛkt] *v.* 檢查；審視

finished [`fɪnɪʃt] *adj.* 完成的；製好的

ship [ʃɪp] *v.* 送貨；運送

efficient [ɪ`fɪʃənt] *adj.* 有效率的

2.2 Continuing the Tour

John and Terry are continuing their tour of the Trenix produc-
tion facilities.

Terry: I didn't know your staff was so large.

John: Trenix employs a total workforce of almost two hundred workers. We're one of the major employers in the region.

Terry: Do they all live on-site?

John: Most of them do. Having our dormitories located so close to the factory spares the staff a long commute. It's much more convenient for them.

Terry: It must pay off for the company, too.

John: Of course—not having to transport workers to the job site helps us keep costs down.

Terry: And probably makes the whole operation more efficient as well.

John: That's right. If you've seen enough here, let's take a look at the sales and marketing department next.

繼續行程

約翰和泰瑞繼續他們參觀川尼斯生產設備的行程。

泰瑞：我不知道你們的員工這麼多。

約翰：川尼斯雇用的員工總人數幾乎達兩百位。我們是本區主要企業主之一。

泰瑞：他們全都住在廠區嗎？

約翰：大部分是。我們的宿舍位離工廠非常近，免去員工長途通勤之勞，對他們而言方便很多。

泰瑞：對公司也一定有利。

約翰：當然——不必接送員工到工作地點幫助我們減低成本。。

泰瑞：而且應該也讓整個營運更有效率。

約翰：沒錯。假如這裡您已經看得差不多了，接下來我們去看業務行銷部。

Word List

production [prə`dʌkʃən] *n.* 生產；製作

staff [stæf] *n.* 全體職員；員工

employer [ɪm`plɔɪɚ] *n.* 雇主

on-site [`ɑn ,saɪt] *adv.* 場內地 （反義字爲 off-site [`ɔf ,saɪt] 場外地）

dormitory [`dɔrmə,torɪ] *n.* （=dorm）宿舍；團體寢室

spare [spɛr] *v.* 使……免於；免除；省掉

commute [kə`mjut] *v./n.* 通勤

pay off [,pe `ɔf] *phr. v.* 使……得益；有報償

3 Biz 加分句型 Nice-to-Know Phrases

 CD I-24

3.1 談論員工 Talking About the Staff

❶ We firmly believe that.... （談論環境、政策時）

我們堅信……。

例 We firmly believe that a happy worker is a <u>productive</u> worker.

我們堅信一個快樂的員工才會是一個具生產力的員工。

❷ We offer.... （談論待遇時）

我們提供……。

例 We offer <u>competitive</u> wages and <u>benefits</u>.

我們提供極具競爭力的薪資和福利。

❸ We <u>draw</u> most of our workforce from.... （談論擇員地區時）

我們的員工大部分選自……。

例 We draw most of our workforce from the area.

我們的員工大部分選自本地區。

❹ Our company offers.... （談論公司制度時）

我們公司提供……。

例 Our company offers many <u>opportunities</u> for <u>advancement</u>.

我們公司提供很多升遷的機會。

Word List

productive [prə`dʌktɪv] *adj.* 具生產力的；
富有成效的
competitive [kəm`pɛtətɪv] *adj.* 具競爭力
的；競爭性的
benefit [`bɛnəfɪt] *n.* 福利；利益

draw [drɔ] *v.* 取自；畫；拉
opportunity [ˌɑpə`tjunətɪ] *n.* 機會；良機
advancement [əd`vænsmənt] *n.* 升遷；進
展；促進推廣

3.2 討論報酬與生產力
Discussing <u>Compensation</u> and <u>Productivity</u>

❶ I should point out that....（吸引客人注意時）

我應該指出……。

例 I should point out that we offer the highest wages in the area.

我應該指出我們提供本地區最高薪資。

❷ You're absolutely right—we've found that....（同意客人看法時）

您完全正確——我們的確發現……。

例 You're absolutely right—we've found that improving benefits also improves productivity.

您完全正確——我們的確發現改善福利的同時也改善了生產力。

❸ On the <u>contrary,</u> we've actually found that....（不贊同客人看法時）

相反地，我們實際發現……。

例 On the contrary, we've actually found that increasing <u>overtime</u> hurts productivity

相反地，我們實際發現延長加班有損生產力。

❹ It<u>'s worth</u> nothing that....（提出見解時）

……是毫無效益的。

例 It's worth nothing that our company offers full <u>insurance</u> coverage for all employees.

我們公司提供所有員工全套保險是毫無效益的。

Ⓦord List

compensation [ˌkɑmpənˈseʃən] *n.* 薪水；津貼

productivity [ˌprodʌkˈtɪvətɪ] *n.* 生產力

contrary [ˈkɑntrɛrɪ] *adj.* 相反的；對立的（on the contrary 相反地）

overtime [ˈovɚˌtaɪm] *n.* 加班；（比賽）延長時間

be worth N/V-ing 值得……

insurance [ɪnˈʃʊrəns] *n.* 保險；保險費

4 Biz 加分字彙 Nice-to-Know Vocabulary

CD I-25

1. **biotech** [`baɪotɛk] *n.* (=biotechnology) 生物科技

2. **nonprofit** [ˌnɑn`prɑfɪt] *n.* 非營利機構；*adj.* 非營利的

3. **wholesale** [`hol,sel] *n.* 批發

4. **logistics** [lo`dʒɪstɪks] *n.*（複數形）物流；後勤

5. **hospitality** [ˌhɑspɪ`tælətɪ] *n.* 餐旅業；殷勤招待

6. **pharmaceutical** [ˌfɑrmə`sjutɪk!] *adj.* 製藥的

7. **computer peripherals** [kəm`pjutɚ pə`rɪfərəls] *n.*（常用複數）電腦週邊設備

8. **job orientation** [`dʒɑb ˌorɪɛn`teʃən] *n.* 新進員工訓練

9. **probation** [pro`beʃən] *n.* 試用期

10. **commission** [kə`mɪʃən] *n.* 佣金

11. **pension** [`pɛnʃən] *n.* 退休金；撫恤金

12. **profit sharing** [`prɑfɪt `ʃɛrɪŋ] *n.* 分紅

13. **flexible working hours** [`flɛksəb! `wɝkɪŋ `aʊrs] *n.* 彈性工時

14. **job rotation** [`dʒɑb ro`teʃən] *n.* 工作輪調

15. **tuition assistance** [tju`ɪʃən ə`sɪstəns] *n.* 學費輔助

:::::::: 小心陷阱 ::::::::

☹ 錯誤用法

Our factory uses **state-of-art** technology.

我們工廠採用先進的科技。

☺ 正確用法

Our factory uses **state-of-the-art** technology.

我們工廠採用先進的科技。

:::::::: 文化小叮嚀 ::::::::

Workplace standards <u>regarding</u> safety often vary from country to country. Before taking a guest on a tour of your operation, <u>it pays to</u> do your own safety inspection to make sure that any potential safety <u>hazards</u> are repaired or removed before your guests arrive. And of course, if warranted, ensure that your guests are provided with the necessary protective <u>gear</u> or clothing (safety <u>goggles</u>, <u>hardhat</u>, ear protection etc.) that is clean and in good repair.

職場的安全標準往往因國家不同而有所不同。在帶訪客踏上參觀作業行程之前，做好安全檢查以確定任何潛在的安全危害已在客人蒞臨前被修復或排除是值得的。而且當然，如果有必要的話，應確保你的客人獲供必要、乾淨、維修狀況良好的防護裝備或衣物（安全防護鏡、工地帽、護耳器等）。

Word List

regarding [rɪ`gardɪŋ] *prep.* 有關

it pays to do sth. 做某事是值得的

hazard [`hæzɚd] *n.* 危險；危害

gear [gɪr] *n.* 特定用途的衣著裝備；工具

goggles [`gɑg[z] *n.*（複數形）護目鏡

hardhat [`hɑrd`hæt] *n.* 工地帽

5 實戰演練 Practice Exercises

Ⅰ 請為下列兩題選出最適本章的中文譯義。

1 talk shop

(A) 論商店 (B) 聊天室 (C) 討論相關業務

2 nuts and bolts

(A) 瑣事雜項 (B) 理論元素 (C) 基本要點

Ⅱ 你會如何回應下面這兩句話?

1 It must pay off for the company, too.

(A) Of course—the savings are substantial.

(B) Yes, we pay off everyone in town, including the police.

(C) Yes, our workers are paid every second Friday.

2 We offer competitive wages and benefits.

(A) It's all about survival of the fittest.

(B) The working conditions here seem quite good too.

(C) Your workers seem to enjoy competing with each other.

Ⅲ 你正帶著一群人參觀你們的巧克力工廠。你想指出你們使用很多海外進口的原料,並密切注意各項生產環節以確保生產最高品質的巧克力。請利用下列詞語寫出一篇簡短的對話:

stringent quality controls	ensure	import a lot of
insist on	incorporate them into	recipes

＊解答請見 231 頁

第 **7** 章

購物
Shopping

Guests will often be interested in a shopping excursion. The prices of consumer goods in Asian countries often represent a substantial savings in comparison to those of Western countries. What's more, many products available where you live will undoubtedly have a distinctly Asian flavor that will appeal to a foreign guest's desire to return home with exotic gifts and souvenirs.

訪客常會對購物行程感興趣。亞洲國家的消費品物價與西方國家的相較起來往往可以省下很多錢;更重要的是,許多在你住的地方可以買到的產品無疑地具有獨特的亞洲風味,常能引發外國訪客想帶些異國風味的禮物和紀念品回家的慾望。

1 Biz 必通句型 Need-to-Know Phrases

 CD I-26

1.1 逛到不行為止 Shop 'Til You Drop

最好先了解客人想要買什麼。

---

❶ Are you in the market for...?
您想買……嗎？
例 Are you in the market for a digital camera?
您想買數位相機嗎？

---

❷ Prices on (product) are (adj.) than they were (time period)
（產品）的價格比（時期）更（形容詞）。
例 Prices on flat-screen TVs are much lower than they were at this time last year.
平面電視的價格比去年的這個時候低多了。

訪客可能不清楚該如何議價或是該要求多少折扣，你應該給一些意見。

---

❸ You (can/can't) bargain here—the prices (are/aren't) negotiable.
這裡（可以／不能）議價──價錢（可以／沒得）商量。
例 You can bargain here—the prices are negotiable.
這裡可以議價──價錢可以商量。

---

❹ I wouldn't pay more than (percentage) of the asking price if I were you.
如果是我的話，超過要價的（百分比）我就不會買。
例 I wouldn't pay more than sixty percent of the asking price if I were you.
如果是我的話，超過要價的六成我就不會買。

---

ord List

be in the market for sth. 想買某物
bargain [`bɑrgɪn] v. 議價

negotiable [nɪ`goʃɪəbl] adj. 可協商的
percentage [pə`sɛntɪdʒ] n. 百分比

⑤ This place has a great <u>selection</u> of....

這裡有很多精選的……。

例 This place has a great selection of local wood <u>carvings</u>.

這裡有很多精選的本地木雕。

一般都是客人自己決定，但必要時可以提供一些衷心的建議。

⑥ (Product) is on sale—it's (percentage) off.

（產品）在特價——（百分比）優惠。

例 This DVD player is on sale—it's thirty percent off.

這款 DVD 播放機在特價——打七折。

⑦ It's a good chance to <u>stock up</u> on....

現在是多買點……的好機會。

例 It's a good chance to stock up on batteries.

現在是多買點電池的好機會。

客人選定後可能需要你的協助。

⑧ I'll ask if they have (it/them) in....

我來問他們（這個／這些）有沒有……。

例 I'll ask if they have it in your size.

我來問問他們這件有沒有適合您的尺寸。

ord List

selection [səˋlɛkʃən] *n.* 精選品；選擇
carving [ˋkɑrvɪŋ] *n.* 雕刻品
stock up [͵stɑkˋʌp] *phr. v.* 囤積

87

1.2 消費者當心 Buyer Beware

你應該帶客人去價格最划算或是有特殊、新奇貨品在特賣的商店。

❶ **This shop has (some of) the best deals <u>around</u> on (product).**

這家店賣（一些）現有價錢最便宜的（產品）。

例 This shop has some of the best deals around on men's shoes.

這家店賣一些現有價錢最划算的男鞋。

❷ **Maybe you can pick up something for (person) in here.**

也許您可以在這裡買點東西給（人）。

例 Maybe you can pick up something for your wife in here.

也許您可以在這裡買點東西給尊夫人。

很多商店都提供訂製貨品郵寄海外的服務。

❸ **You can have... made <u>to order</u>.**

您可以訂做（東西）。

例 You can have a silk suit made to order.

您可以訂做一套絲質西裝。

❹ **They will ship... to....**

他們會將……寄到……。

例 The artist says they will ship the painting to your home in Germany.

畫家說他們會將畫寄到您德國的府上。

Word List

around [əˈraʊnd] *adj.* 現有的   to order 依照指示規格

如果你的客人不久就要離開的話，他們應該選擇有國際保固的產品。

---

❺ (They offer/It comes with) a (time period) <u>warranty</u>.
（他們提供／它有）（期限）的保固。
例 They offer a one-year warranty.
他們提供一年的保固。

---

❻ The warranty <u>covers</u>/doesn't cover....
保固涵蓋／不涵蓋……。
例 The warranty covers <u>parts</u> and service.
保固涵蓋零件和服務。

店員不一定能和你的客人溝通，你應該適時地挺"聲"相助。

---

❼ You can try it on—there's a <u>fitting room</u> (location).
您可以試穿看看──（地方）有試衣間。
例 You can try it on—there's a fitting room over there.
您可以試穿看看──那裡有試衣間。

---

❽ Are you looking for a <u>specific</u> (brand/<u>label</u>/designer etc.)?
您在找特定的（品牌／牌子／設計師等）嗎？
例 Are you looking for a specific brand?
您在找特定的品牌嗎？

Word **L**ist

warranty [ˋwɔrəntɪ] *n.* 保固
cover [ˋkʌvɚ] *v.* 包含；覆蓋
part [pɑrt] *n.* 零件；部分
fitting room [ˋfɪtɪŋ ˏrum] *n.* 試衣間

specific [spɪˋsɪfɪk] *adj.* 特定的；具體的
label [ˋlebl] *n.* （紙、布或塑膠等材質的）標籤；品牌

89

2 實戰會話 Show Time

 CD I-27

2.1 Hunting for Deals

Terry has asked John if he might be able to do some shopping. It's his first trip to Taiwan and he'd like to look at <u>electronics</u>. John has offered to go with him.

John: Are you in the market for souvenirs?

Terry: Not today—I can get those later. I'd really like to look at some digital cameras.

John: You're in the right place. (*<u>Gesturing</u> and leading him to a shop.*) This place has a great selection of digital cameras.

Terry: Wow! I can see that. I've never seen so many electronic stores in one place! Aren't the stores afraid of competition?

John: It's common in Taiwan for stores of a certain type to be located together. It makes it easy for shoppers to <u>compare</u> prices. Are you looking for a specific <u>make</u>?

Terry: Not really. Just for something with the <u>features</u> I want that's in my price <u>range</u>.

John: It's a good time to buy. Prices on digitals are much lower than they were a couple of years ago. What about this one? This camera is on sale—it's twenty percent off.

譯文

搜尋目標

泰瑞問約翰他是否能夠去買點東西。這是他第一次到台灣，想看看電子產品。約翰表示願意陪他去。

約翰：您想買紀念品嗎？

泰瑞：今天不想——紀念品我可以晚點再買。我很想看看數位相機。

約翰：您來對地方了。（*作勢帶他前往一家店*）這裡有很多精選的數位相機。

泰瑞：哇！我看到了。我從來沒看過一個地方有這麼多電子用品店的！這些店不怕競爭嗎？

約翰：在台灣特定種類的店聚集在一起是很普遍的，這讓顧客容易比價。您在找特定的機型嗎？

泰瑞：其實沒有。我在找有我想要的功能而且在我預算之內的。

約翰：現在買正是時候，數位產品的價格比幾年前低多了。這台怎麼樣？這款相機正在特價——打八折。

Word List

electronics [ɪlɛk`trɑnɪks] *n.*（不可數）電子產品
gesture [`dʒɛstʃɚ] *v.* 作勢；動作示意（尤其是手部與頭部）
compare [kəm`pɛr] *v.* 比較；對照
make [mek] *n.* 型號；品牌
feature [fitʃɚ] *n.* 特點；特徵
range [rendʒ] *n.* 範圍；幅度

2.2 Sizing Up Some Threads

Terry got the digital camera he wanted. Now he's looking for some good deals on clothes.

Terry: Do you mind if we take a look in here?

John: Of course not. I should tell you before we go in, you can bargain here—the prices are negotiable.

Terry: That seems to be the case in many places in Asia. I really had trouble getting used to it at first, though—most stores where I'm from have fixed prices.

John: It's part of the culture! I wouldn't pay more than half of the asking price if I were you.

Terry: Really? I thought that 10 or 20 percent was a normal discount?

John: It depends on the place. That's true for department stores, but for local shops like this one, there's room for bargaining.

Terry: (*Looking at some trousers*). I like these, but I'm not crazy about the color.

John: I'll ask them if they have them in another color.

挑選衣衫

泰瑞買了他想要的數位相機。現在他在找幾件划算的衣服。

泰瑞：你介意我們逛一下這裡嗎？

約翰：當然不。在我們進去之前，我應該先告訴您，這裡可以議價——價錢能商量。

泰瑞：亞洲好像有很多地方都是這樣。雖然一開始時我真的很難習慣——我來的地方大部分的商店都有固定的價格。

約翰：這是文化的一部分！如果是我的話，超過要價的五成我就不會買。

泰瑞：真的？我還以為九折或八折是正常的折扣？

約翰：這要看地方。百貨公司是這樣沒錯，但在本地商店像這家，是有議價空間的。

泰瑞：（*看著幾條褲子*）我喜歡這些，但顏色我不怎麼喜歡。

約翰：我來問他們這些褲子有沒有其他顏色。

Word List

size up [ˌsaɪz ˋʌp] *phr. v.* 打量；思考判斷

threads [θrɛdz] *n.* （俚語，複數形）衣物（＝clothes）

have trouble doing sth. 做某事有困難

fixed [fɪkst] *adj.* 固定的；不動的

normal [ˋnɔrml] *adj.* 正常的；標準的

trousers [ˋtrauzɚz] *n.* （複數形）褲子（a pair of trousers 一條褲子）

be crazy about sth. 非常熱衷某事物

3 Biz 加分句型 Nice-to-Know Phrases

CD I-28

3.1 談論品質與供應
Talking About Quality and <u>Availability</u>

❶ Always check....
一定要檢查……。
例 Always check the quality carefully before you buy.
購買之前一定要仔細檢查品質。

❷ It looks to me like....
我覺得看起來……。
例 It looks to me like the <u>workmanship</u> is a little <u>shoddy</u>.
我覺得這手工看起來有點粗糙。

❸ That brand (has/doesn't have) a reputation for....
那個牌子（有／沒有）……的信譽。
例 That brand has a good reputation for quality.
那個牌子的品質有良好的信譽。

❹ They're <u>out of</u> <u>stock</u>.
它們現在缺貨。
例 They're out of stock, but they have another <u>model</u> in stock.
它們現在缺貨，但他們另一種型號有存貨。

Ⓦord List

availability [ə‚velə`bɪlətɪ] *n.* 可得性；可利用性

workmanship [`wɝkmən‚ʃɪp] *n.* 手藝；細工

shoddy [`ʃɑdɪ] *adj.* 品質不佳的

out of [`aut‚ɑv] *prep.* 賣完；用光

stock [stɑk] *n.* 貯存；存貨

model [`mɑdḷ] *n.* 型號；樣式

3.2 盜版和仿冒品 Pirated and Knock-off Goods

❶ This/that (product) has been pirated—it....

這個／那個（產品）被盜版了——它……。

例 That VCD has been pirated—it's not a licensed product.

那個VCD被盜版了——它不是個授權的產品。

❷ Be wary of....

小心……。

例 Be wary of knockoffs. They may be cheap, but the quality might not be very good.

要小心仿冒品。它們或許便宜，但品質可能不太好。

❸ Piracy is still a problem here,....

盜版還是這裡的問題，……。

例 Unfortunately, piracy is still a problem here. But the authorities are cracking down.

令人遺憾的是，這裡還是有盜版的問題。不過主管機關已經在取締了。

❹ If you get caught with pirated goods,....

如果你攜帶盜版品被抓，……。

例 If you get caught with pirated goods, you could be fined.

如果你攜帶盜版品被抓，你可能會被罰錢。

Ｗord List

pirated [`paɪrətɪd] *adj.* 盜版的（動詞為 pirate）

knock(-)off [`nɑk ˌɔf] *adj.* 仿冒的；*n.* 仿冒品

licensed [`laɪsn̩st] *adj.* 經過授權的；獲得許可的

be wary of N./V-ing 謹防……；小心……

authority [ə`θɔrətɪ] *n.* 權力；權威（the authorities 官方；當局）

crack down [ˌkræk `daʊn] *phr. v.* 取締；壓制

4 Biz 加分字彙 Nice-to-Know Vocabulary

 CD I-29

❶ discount store [ˋdɪskaʊnt ˋstor] *n.* 折扣店

❷ specialty store [ˋspɛʃəltɪ ˋstor] *n.* 專門店

❸ tailor-make [ˌteləˋmek] *v.* 特製；訂做

❹ outlet [ˋaʊtˌlɛt] *n.* 暢貨中心

❺ closeout [ˋklozˌaʊt] *n.* 出清拍賣；清倉銷售

❻ camcorder [ˋkæmˌkɔrdə] *n.* 攝錄像機

❼ desktop [ˋdɛsktɑp] *n.* 桌上型電腦

❽ coupon [ˋkupɑn] *n.* 優待卷；兌換卷

❾ flaw [flɔ] *n.* 瑕疵；缺點

❿ return [rɪˋtɝn] *n.* 退貨

⓫ exchange [ɪksˋtʃendʒ] *v./n.* 更換；兌換

⓬ reimbursement [ˌriimˋbɝsmənt] *n.* 退款；補償

⓭ credit [ˋkrɛdɪt] *n.* 抵減額；賒帳；信用

⓮ shipping charge [ˋʃɪpɪŋ ˋtʃɑrdʒ] *n.* 運費

⓯ tax refund [ˋtæks ˋrɪˌfʌnd] *n.* 退稅

:::::::: 小心陷阱 ::::::::

☹ 錯誤用法

You'll have to **chat with** the shopkeeper if you want to get a good deal.

如果你想拿到好價錢的話，你必須和店家議價。

☺ 正確用法

You'll have to **bargain with** the shopkeeper if you want to get a good deal.

如果你想拿到好價錢的話，你必須和店家議價。

:::::::: 文化小叮嚀 ::::::::

Bargaining may or may not be common where you live. If your guest is uncomfortable with bargaining, common courtesy says that you should offer to <u>do battle with</u> the shopkeeper <u>on your guest's behalf</u>.

Pirated goods may or may not be a problem where you live. Be aware that many Westerners <u>take a dim view towards</u> piracy and may <u>take issue with</u> any comments that suggest easy access to pirated goods is somehow a good thing.

議價在你居住的地方不一定是常態。如果你的客人對於討價還價不自在，依一般禮貌，你應該出面幫客人和店家交涉。

盜版品在你居住的地方不一定是個問題。需注意很多西方人不贊同盜版的行為，並且可能會對任何暗示「容易買到盜版品其實不錯」這樣的評論提出異議。

Word List

do battle with.... 對抗……；與……作戰

on/in someone's behalf 代表某人（亦可用 on/in behalf of someone）

take a dim view towards... 不贊同……（dim [dɪm] *adj.* 昏暗的；模糊的）

take issue with... 對……提出異議（issue [ˈɪʃju] *n.* 議題；爭論）

5 實戰演練 Practice Exercises

I 請為下列三題選出最適本章的中文譯義。

❶ in the market for...

(A) 上市場買…… (B) 想買…… (C) 採購……

❷ not crazy about

(A)不特別喜歡…… (B) 不對……生氣 (C) 不對……上癮

❸ crack down

(A) 打破 (B) 取締 (C) 解開

II 你會如何回應下面這兩句話？

❶ They're out of stock.

(A) Great—I'll take three!

(B) That's too bad.

(C) They should sit down and take a rest.

❷ I'm looking for a specific brand.

(A) I used to play in a band, too.

(B) Which brand?

(C) Must you be so picky?

III 你帶一位客人逛本地的骨董市場，你想告訴他／她和店家議價的常見方法。請利用下列詞語寫出一篇簡短的解說：

I should tell you	bargain	prices are negotiable
pay more than	asking price	if I were you	two-thirds

＊解答請見 232 頁

第 8 章

上 KTV
At the KTV

A trip to a reputable and classy KTV (karaoke) is a popular night out for business people throughout Asia. Never underestimate the value of song—music is a universal language that can go a long way towards breaking down cultural barriers.

去一趟名聲好且精緻的 KTV（卡拉 OK）是很受亞洲各地商業人士歡迎的一項夜間外出活動。不要低估歌唱的價值——音樂是全球共通的語言，對於打破文化隔閡非常有效。

1 Biz 必通句型 Need-to-Know Phrases

1.1 介紹 KTV 文化 Introducing the KTV Culture　　CD I-30

KTV 在西方國家的人氣遠不如亞洲國家，如果你的客人不清楚 KTV 是什麼的話，應該稍微說明一下。

---

❶ **(Something) is really popular with (somebody) in (some place).**
（某事）在（某地）非常受（某人）的歡迎。
例 KTV is really popular with students and business people in Taiwan.
KTV 在台灣非常受學生和商業人士的歡迎。

---

❷ **This will be a great chance for you to....**
這將是你……的好機會。
例 This will be a great chance for you to see how Chinese people <u>unwind</u> after a hard day.
這將是你看看中國人如何在辛苦一天後放鬆的好機會。

---

❸ **The songs are mostly in (language), but they have (language) songs, too.**
歌曲大部分都是（語言）的，但他們也有（語言）歌曲。
例 The songs are mostly in Mandarin, but they have English songs, too.
大部分都是國語歌曲，但他們也有英文歌曲。

進 KTV 後，下列這五句話能讓氣氛輕鬆一點。

---

❹ **We can order... to the room.**
我們可以點……到包廂。
例 We can order food and cigarettes to the room.
我們可以點食物和香菸到包廂。

---

ord List

unwind [ʌn`waɪnd] *v.* 放鬆；鬆開

❺ Have a look at... and see if there is/are... you'd like to....

看一下……，看看有沒有你想……的……。

例 Have a look at the songbook and see if there are some songs you'd like to sing.

看一下歌本，看看有沒有你想唱的歌。

❻ It's a private room, so you don't have to worry about....

這是私人包廂，所以你不必擔心……。

例 It's a private room, so you don't have to worry about having to listen to strangers <u>butcher</u> the <u>classics</u>.

這是私人包廂，所以你不必擔心必須聽陌生人活生生糟蹋經典好歌。

❼ Have a seat. Make yourself (adj.)

請坐，讓自己（形容詞）。

例 Have a seat. Make yourself comfortable.

請坐，讓自己舒適一點。

❽ Who is your favorite (<u>band</u>, singer, musician, etc.)?

你最喜歡的（團體、歌手、音樂家等）是誰？

例 Who is your favorite band?

你最喜歡的樂團是哪一個？

ord List

butcher [ˈbutʃɚ] *v.* 弄糟；屠殺
classic [ˈklæsɪk] *n.* 經典之作；傑作
band [ˈbænd] *n.* 群；團體；樂團；樂隊

2.2 音準演出 Hitting the <u>Note</u>

大部分的人對於自己的歌聲多少都會有點害羞，適時地給予客人讚美能讓氣氛更融洽。

❶ I had no idea (somebody) was/were such a(n)....
我不知道（某人）是這樣的⋯⋯。
例 I had no idea you were such a talented singer.
我不知道您是這麼有天分的唱將。

❷ That was a (really) (adj.) <u>rendition</u> of that song.
剛才那首歌詮釋地（真得）（形容詞）。
例 That was a really <u>touching</u> rendition of that song.
剛才那首歌詮釋地真是動人。

❸ (Somebody's) voice is very (adj.)
（某人的）聲音非常（形容詞）。
例 Your voice is very strong.
您的聲音非常渾厚。

❹ Listen to (somebody). He/She can really....
聽一下（某人）。他／她真的很會⋯⋯。
例 Listen to Shelly! She can really <u>belt</u> it <u>out</u>!
聽雪莉唱！她真的很會飆歌！

Ⓦord List

note [not] *n.* 音；音符
rendition [rɛn`dɪʃən] *n.* 表演；詮釋
touching [`tʌtʃɪŋ] *adj.* 動人的；感人的
belt out [ˌbɛlt `aut] *phr. v.* 大聲唱

唱不好某首歌的時候，可以說下面這句話。

❺ This song is (a little) too (adj.) for me.
這首歌對我來說（有點）太（形容詞）。
例 This song is a little too high for me. I can't hit all the notes.
這首歌對我來說有點太高，有些音我唱不上去。

❻ (Somebody) is always <u>hogging</u> the....
（某人）總是抓著（某物）不放。
例 Grace is always hogging the <u>microphone</u>. She's a real <u>diva</u>!
葛蕾斯總是抓著麥克風不放。她真的是個歌后！

❼ Please pass me....
請把……遞給我。
例 Please pass me the <u>remote control</u>.
請把遙控器遞給我。

即使最愛唱歌的人，到最後也會沒有力氣。

❽ Have you had enough (V-ing) for one night?
一個晚上……你覺得夠了嗎？
例 What do you say, Terry? Have you had enough singing for
one night?
你怎麼樣，泰瑞？一個晚上唱下來你覺得夠了嗎？

ord List

hog [hɑg] *v.* 霸佔；獨佔
microphone [`maɪkrə‚fon] *n.* 麥克風 (=mike, mic)
diva [`divə] *n.* （歌劇的）女主唱
remote control [rɪ`mot kən`trol] *n.* 遙控器

2 實戰會話 Show Time

CD I-31

2.1 Going to the KTV

John and Terry have <u>wrapped up</u> a day of meetings and it's time to go out and <u>blow off</u> some <u>steam</u>. The plan is to go to a nearby KTV to meet staff from the office.

Terry: So, John, you say we're going to <u>karaoke</u> tonight?

John: Yeah. KTV is really popular with business people in Taiwan.

Terry: I've heard that, but... I think maybe I should get back to the hotel for some rest.

John: Oh, come on, Terry! This will be a great chance for you to see how we unwind after a hard day.

Terry: OK, but I'm warning you: I'm <u>not much of a</u> singer.

John: Don't worry—it's a private room so you don't have to worry about singing in front of <u>total</u> strangers. You'll be among friends!

Terry: But I can't read Chinese! How can I sing?

John: No problem—the songs are mostly in Mandarin, but they have English songs, too.

Terry: Do I get a prize or anything if I sing well?

John: No, you get something even more important: face!

譯 文

上 KTV

約翰和泰瑞剛結束一整天的會，這會兒該是出去宣洩一下的時候了。他們計劃到附近的一家 KTV 和辦公室的人碰頭。

泰瑞：所以，約翰，你說我們今天晚上要去卡拉 OK？

約翰：是啊。KTV 在台灣非常受商業人士的歡迎。

泰瑞：我聽說過，但……我想也許我應該回飯店休息。

約翰：噢，拜託，泰瑞！這將是您看看我們如何在辛苦一天後放鬆的好機會。

泰瑞：好吧，但我先警告你：我不怎麼會唱歌。

約翰：別擔心——是私人包廂，所以您不必擔心要在完全陌生的人面前唱歌。您的周圍都會是朋友！

泰瑞：可是我看不懂中文！我要怎麼唱？

約翰：沒問題——雖然大部分都是國語歌曲，但他們也有英文歌。

泰瑞：我唱得好的話有獎品或什麼東西嗎？

約翰：沒有，但您得到更重要的：面子！

Word List

wrap up [ˌræp ˋʌp] *phr. v.* 結束；完成

blow off steam [ˌblɔ ˋɔf ˋstim] （非正式）宣洩積壓的情緒

karaoke [ˌkɑrɑˋoke] *n.* 卡拉 OK（由日文カラオケ英譯而來）

not much of a N. 並不是個太好的……；稱不上是個……

total [ˋtotl] *adj.* 完全的；絕對的

2.2 Hitting the Note

One of the girls from accounting, Gina, is belting out a <u>number</u> to the <u>delight</u> of her colleagues. John and Terry are <u>critiquing</u> her performance.

Terry: I had no idea Gina was such a talented singer.

John: She's amazing!

Terry: <u>Tell me about it</u>. Her voice is very strong, especially for her size.

John: We have another microphone if you'd like to join in.

Terry: This song is a little too difficult for me. I could never <u>pull it off</u>!

John: Me neither. (*Clapping.*) Nice job, Gina! That was a really <u>stirring</u> rendition of that song.

Terry: Ahhh...here's one I like. It's an old Beatles song that I remember from when I was growing up. John, please pass me the remote control.

John: (*Handing the remote to Terry.*) Here you are. But aren't most Beatles songs from the 60s?

Terry: I'm older than you think, John!

譯文

音準演出

會計部的一個女孩，吉娜，正在飆一首歌娛樂她的同事。約翰和泰瑞正在評論她的表現。

泰瑞：我不知道吉娜是這麼有天分的唱將。

約翰：她很厲害！

泰瑞：我知道。她的聲音非常渾厚，尤其以她的體型來說。

約翰：如果您想加入的話，我們有另一支麥克風。

泰瑞：這首歌對我來說有點太難，我絕對不可能唱好的！

約翰：我也不行。（*拍手*）唱得好，吉娜！剛才那首歌詮釋地真是太動人了。

約翰：啊……這裡有首我喜歡的歌，一首從我成長開始就記得的披頭四老歌。約翰，請把遙控器遞給我。

約翰：（*把遙控器遞給泰瑞*）給您。但披頭四的歌大部分不都來自六〇年代嗎？

泰瑞：我比你想的還要老，約翰！

Word List

number [`nʌmbɚ] *n.* 一段音樂；一首歌曲
delight [dɪ`laɪt] *n.* 愉悅；快樂（to the delight of someone 使某人高興）
critique [krɪ`tik] *v.* 評論；批評
Tell me about it. 說得對；我知道（或是 Tell me.）
pull off sth. 成功完成某事；成功做了某難事
clap [klæp] *v.* 拍手；鼓掌
stirring [`stɝɪŋ] *adj.* 激動人心的

3 Biz 加分句型 Nice-to-Know Phrases

CD I-28

3.1 討論某首歌時
When You're Talking About a Song

❶ This is a cover of a(n) (name) song.
這是一首（名稱）的翻唱歌。
例 This is a <u>cover</u> of a Temptations song.
這是一首「誘惑合唱團」的翻唱歌。

❷ I always preferred the... <u>version</u> of this song.
這首歌我始終比較喜歡……的版本。
例 I always preferred the Diana Ross version of this song.
這首歌我始終比較喜歡黛安娜・蘿絲唱的版本。

❸ This song was a big <u>hit</u> (number) years ago.
這首歌（數字）年前非常紅。
例 This song was a big hit about twenty years ago.
這首歌大約 20 年前非常紅。

❹ This song was popular when....
這首歌在……時相當受歡迎。
例 This song was popular when I was in high school.
這首歌在我唸中學時很流行。

Word List

cover [ˋkʌvɚ] *n.* 翻唱歌；*v.* 翻唱
version [ˋvɝʒən] *n.* 版本
hit [hɪt] *n.* 受歡迎的熱門事物；成功而風行一時的事物

3.2 討論某種音樂類型時 Talking About a Style of Music

討論有助拉近彼此的距離，下列這四句可用來表達你的喜好與想法。

❶ I'm really not <u>into</u>....（表示不喜歡某種音樂時）
我實在對……沒有興趣。
例 I'm really not into boy bands.
我實在對男孩團體沒有興趣。

❷ I'm a <u>sucker for</u>....（表示對某種音樂的喜愛時）
我是……迷。
例 I'm a sucker for romantic <u>ballads</u>.
我是浪漫抒情歌迷。

❸ ... is really popular these days.
最近……非常流行。
例 Electronic dance music is really popular these days.
最近電子舞曲真得很流行。

❹ ... is <u>all the rage</u> now, but....
……現在超級熱門，但……。
例 Rap is all the rage now, but it's just not my thing.
饒舌樂現在超級熱門，但那不是我喜歡的種類。

Word List

be into sth. 對某事物很感興趣

be a sucker for... 因非常喜歡而無法抗拒……的迷（sucker [ˋsʌkɚ] n. 吸盤；易受騙的呆瓜）

ballad [ˋbæləd] n. 浪漫情歌；芭樂歌

sth. is (all) the rage 某事物非常熱門、受歡迎

4 Biz 加分字彙 Nice-to-Know Vocabulary

 CD I-33

❶ **monitor** [`manətɚ] *n.* 螢幕（或用 screen 和 display）

❷ **tambourine** [ˌtæmbə`rin] *n.* 鈴鼓

❸ **maracas** [mə`rækəz] *n.* 沙鈴

❹ **throat lozenge** [`θrot `lazɪndʒ] *n.* 喉糖

❺ **chorus** [`korəs] *n.* 副歌；合唱；合唱隊

❻ **duet** [du`ɛt] *n.* 雙人合唱曲；二重奏

❼ **off-key** [ˌɔf`ki] *adj.* 走音的；*adv.* 走音地

❽ **sing in tune** 唱準音（tune [tjun] *n.* 音調；歌曲）

❾ **sing out of tune** 唱走音

❿ **mellow** [`mɛlo] *adj.* （聲音）圓潤的

⓫ **raspy** [`ræspɪ] *adj.* （聲音）粗糙沙啞的

⓬ **teenybopper** [`tinɪˌbɑpɚ] *n.* 穿著時髦的少女流行音樂迷

⓭ **bass** [`bes] *n.* 男低音, **alto** [`ælto] *n.* 女低音

⓮ **baritone** [`bærəˌton] *n.* 男中音，
mezzo-soprano [`mɛtso sə`præno] *n.* 女中音

⓯ **tenor** [`tɛnɚ] *n.* 男高音，**soprano** [sə`præno] *n.* 女高音

::::::: 小心陷阱 :::::::

☹ 錯誤用法

This song is very **classical**!

這首歌很經典！

☺ 正確用法

This song is **a classic!**

這首歌很經典！

::::::: 文化小叮嚀 :::::::

Playing <u>finger counting games</u> and drinking numerous <u>toasts</u> are often part of a night out at KTV. Sometimes foreign guests <u>underestimate</u> the effects so many small glasses of beer consumed so quickly will have on their <u>sobriety.</u> Remember to <u>keep an eye on</u> your guest to make sure they're comfortable. And of course, remember to make sure all your guests take a taxi if they've been drinking.

划酒拳和猛乾酒常是夜間 KTV 活動的一部分。有時候外國客人低估這麼快喝下這麼多小杯啤酒對他們的神智所造成的影響，記得隨時注意一下你的客人，以確定他們沒有不適。而且當然，如果客人喝了酒，記得確定他們全都是搭計程車回去的。

Ⓦord List

finger counting game 數字拳；台灣拳（兩者都是猜划拳者手指相加總數，數字拳的出拳基本指數為 0、5、10，台灣拳的則在 0~5 之間，猜對者贏）

toast [tost] *n./v.* 乾杯；敬酒

underestimate [ˈʌndəˈɛstəˌmet] *v.* 低估

sobriety [səˈbraɪətɪ] *n.* 清醒

keep an eye on sb./sth. 注意某人／某事

實戰演練 Practice Exercises

I 請為下列三題選出最適本章的中文譯義。

❶ blow off some steam

(A) 全力以赴 (B) 宣洩一下 (C) 大發雷霆

❷ belt out a number

(A) 高唱一首歌 (B) 大聲叫出號碼 (C) 狂飆一串歌

❸ be into something

(A) 了解某事物 (B) 進入某事物 (C) 熱中某事物

II 你會如何回應下面這兩句話？

❶ Have you had enough singing for one night?

(A) Which night did you have in mind?

(B) Not yet—let's stay a little longer.

(C) I prefer to sing in the daytime.

❷ Have a drink. Make yourself at home.

(A) Thanks, don't mind if I do.

(B) But I don't want to go home yet.

(C) Thanks, but I don't make drinks at home.

III 你跟客人和一群同事在 KTV，一首你最喜歡的歌正要播出，你想發表一下你對 50 年代美國搖滾樂的喜愛。請利用下列詞語寫出你要講的話：

a classic	I'm a sucker for	the oldies
the fifties	rock and roll	these days

＊解答請見 233 頁

夜市
A Night Market

Where else but a night market can visitors get a taste of Asian nightlife that blends eating, shopping, and culture together into one sensory overload? All that fried food may not be the healthiest thing going, but an occasional indulgence can be a real treat.

除了夜市還有哪個地方能讓訪客體驗由飲食、購物與文化混合形成感官盛宴的亞洲夜生活呢？儘管油炸食物不是什麼非常健康的東西，但偶爾放縱一下是個十足的享受。

1 Biz 加分句型 Need-to-Know Phrases

CD II-01

1.1 食物及其烹調方法
The Food and its Preparation

夜市的豐富多樣化很容易讓外國訪客感到迷惘、困惑，所以你必須當個好導遊不斷地解說。

❶ This <u>stall</u> is selling....
這攤在賣⋯⋯。
例 This stall is selling <u>tempura</u>.
這攤在賣天婦羅。

❷ ... is/are <u>dipped</u> in <u>batter</u> before it's/they're fried in oil.
⋯⋯在油炸之前會先沾裹麵糊。
例 The <u>squid</u> are dipped in batter before they're fried in oil.
魷魚在油炸之前會先沾裹麵糊。

❸ These (cakes/<u>dumplings</u>/<u>pastries</u> etc.) have... <u>filling</u> inside.
這些（糕點／餃子麵糰類／酥餅等）有⋯⋯內餡。
例 These cakes have red bean filling inside.
這些糕點有紅豆內餡。

Word List

stall [stɔl] *n.* (展覽) 攤位；展示桌；小隔間
tempura [ˈtɛmˈpʊrə] *n.* 天婦羅（由日文てんぷら英譯而來，將肉類、蔬菜等食材裹粉加以油炸的料理）
dip [dɪp] *v.* 沾；浸
batter [ˈbætə] *n.* 麵糊

squid [skwɪd] *n.* 魷魚
dumpling [ˈdʌmplɪŋ] *n.* 由麵糰製成的小團狀食物（如爲中國料理的話可能是湯圓、餛飩、水餃、蒸餃、小湯包等）
pastry [ˈpestrɪ] *n.* 由水、麵粉、酥油揉成的烘焙用麵糰；酥皮；酥皮糕餅
filling [ˈfɪlɪŋ] *n.* 餡；填充物

❹ **These (cakes/dumplings/pastries etc.) are filled with....**

這些（糕點／餃子麵糰類／酥餅等）裡面填滿了……。

例 These buns are filled with shredded pork.

這些包子裡面填滿了豬絞肉。

很多訪客會想知道這些不同的美食小吃是如何調製的。

❺ **This variety of (food) is boiled in....**

這種（食物）是用……煮的。

例 This variety of egg is boiled in tea.

這種蛋是用茶煮的。【茶葉蛋：tea egg】

❻ **The (food) are barbecued over an open flame.**

這（食物）是直接用火烤的。

例 The sausages are barbecued over an open flame.

這些香腸是直接用火烤的。

❼ **The (food) are roasted in an oven.**

這（食物）是在爐子裡烤的。

例 The chestnuts are roasted in an oven.

這些栗子是在爐子裡烤的。

❽ **This type of (food) is steamed/fried/boiled.**

這種（食物）是蒸／炸／煮的。

例 This type of bread is steamed.

這種麵包是蒸的。

Word List

bun [bʌn] *n.* 夾漢堡、熱狗等的鬆軟麵包；小圓麵包

shredded [`ʃrɛdɪd] *adj.* 絞成碎長狀的（動詞原形為 shred）

boil [bɔɪl] *v.* 煮；煮沸

barbecue [`bɑrbɪˌkju] *v.* 燒烤（常縮寫成 BBQ）

flame [flem] *n.* 火焰

sausage [`sɔsɪdʒ] *n.* 香腸

chestnut [`tʃɛsˌnʌt] *n.* 栗子；栗樹

steamed [stimd] *adj.* 蒸製的（動詞為 steam）

1.2 談論食物與享受美食
Talking About Food and its Enjoyment

交換彼此吃完後的感覺能幫助拉近你和客人的距離。

❶ The (food) <u>melt(s)</u> in your mouth.
這（食物）會在你的嘴裡溶化。
例 The chocolates melt in your mouth.
這巧克力會在你的嘴裡溶化。

❷ ... is/are a little too (adj.) for my taste.
以我的口味來說……有點太（形容詞）了。
例 The <u>glazed</u> strawberries are a little too sweet for my taste.
以我的口味來說冰糖草莓有點太甜了。

❸ I must admit I <u>have a weakness for</u>....
我必須承認我抗拒不了……。
例 I must admit I have a weakness for fried food.
我必須承認我抗拒不了油炸食物。

❹ Eating... at a night market is what you could call a guilty pleasure.
在夜市吃……，可以稱為是「充滿罪惡感的享受」。
例 Eating <u>sweets</u> at a night market is what you could call a guilty pleasure.
在夜市吃甜食，可以稱為是「充滿罪惡感的享受」。

Ⓦord List

melt [mɛlt] *v.* 溶化；熔解；融化
glazed [glezd] *adj.* 淋上透明晶亮糖漿的；上過釉的

have a weakness for sth. 無法抗拒某事物；非常喜歡某事物（weakness [`wiknɪs] *n.* 缺點；弱點；偏愛）
sweets [swits] *n.* （常用複數）甜食

❺ **A trip to the night market isn't complete without eating....**

沒有吃⋯⋯的話就不算逛了夜市。

例 A trip to the night market isn't complete without eating barbequed corn.

沒有吃烤玉米的話就不算逛了夜市。

面對眾多的選擇，你的任務是引領客人前往對的方向。

❻ **You've got to try....**

你一定要試試⋯⋯。

例 You've got to try pork <u>ribs</u> <u>simmered</u> with <u>medicinal</u> herbs.

你一定要試試藥燉排骨。

❼ **... is/are a local <u>delicacy</u>.**

⋯⋯是一道地方佳餚。

例 Duck <u>tongue</u> is a local delicacy.

鴨舌頭是一道本地佳餚。

❽ **(Kind of fruit) is/are <u>in season</u> now.**

（水果種類）正當季。

例 <u>Dragon fruit</u> is in season now.

火龍果正當季。

ord List

rib [rɪb] *n.* 排骨；肋條

simmer [`sɪmɚ] *v.* 煨；燉

medicinal [mə`dɪsn̩l] *adj.* 有藥效的；藥用的

delicacy [`dɛləkəsɪ] *n.* 珍饈佳餚；美味食品

tongue [tʌŋ] *n.* 舌頭；舌肉

in season 當令的；旺季的

dragon fruit [`drægən ˌfrut] *n.* 火龍果（亦稱為 pitaya 或 dragon pearl，原生自中南美洲）

2 實戰會話 Show Time

 CD II-02

2.1 The Food and its Preparation

John and Terry are standing in a crowded night market. Their stomachs are <u>growling</u>, and the sights and smells of all the delicious food are like a <u>siren song</u> neither man can resist.

Terry: What is this, over here?

John: This stall is selling hot dogs.

Terry: Hot dogs? Those look more like <u>corn dogs</u> to me.

John: We call them hot dogs. The <u>wieners</u> are dipped in batter before they're fried in oil.

Terry: I'd prefer something that isn't <u>deep-fried</u>—I'm watching what I eat these days.

John: Fair enough. How about a sausage? The sausages are barbecued over an open flame.

Terry: Yeah, that's more like it. But what..., no buns?

John: No buns—we eat them <u>skewered</u> on a stick!

譯文

食物及其烹調方法

約翰和泰瑞正站在擁擠的夜市裡。他們的肚子正嘰哩咕嚕叫，而眼睛看到的和鼻子聞到的各式美食正如希臘神話女海妖的誘人歌聲，沒有一個抗拒得了。

泰瑞：這邊這個是什麼？

約翰：這攤在賣熱狗。

泰瑞：熱狗？我看起來比較像是炸熱狗。

約翰：我們叫熱狗。維也納香腸在油炸之前會先沾裹麵糊。

泰瑞：我比較喜歡非油炸的食物──最近我很注意吃的東西。

約翰：行。香腸怎麼樣？香腸是直接用火烤的。

泰瑞：好，這比較像話。但是什麼⋯⋯，沒有麵包？

約翰：沒有麵包──我們都是插在竹籤上吃的。

Word List

growl [graʊl] *v.* 咆哮；吼叫

siren song [`saɪrən ˌsɔŋ] *n.* 致命吸引（The Sirens 為希臘神話中居於 Sirenum scopuli 三岩島的人頭鳥身女妖，歌聲美妙迷人，路過的水手往往無法抗拒吸引，因此衝撞岩壁而亡）

corn dog [`kɔrn ˌdɔg] *n.* 裹玉米粉炸成的熱狗

wiener [`winɚ] *n.* 維也納香腸（又叫 frank-furter [`fræŋkfɚtɚ] *n.* 法蘭克福香腸，即沒有裹粉的熱狗）

deep-fried [`dip `fraɪd] *adj.* 油炸的

skewered [`skjuɚd] *adj.* 插入尖頭細長物的（動詞原形為 skewer）

2.2 Talking About Food and its Enjoyment

Terry has finished his sausage, but he's still hungry and there are many foods left to <u>sample</u>. John leads him over to a <u>stinky tofu</u> <u>stand</u>.

John: A trip to the night market isn't complete without eating stinky tofu.

Terry: Oh, no. I was afraid of this moment. I've been warned about "chou dofu."

John: It's quite delicious. Stinky tofu is a local delicacy.

Terry: But that smell....

John: You've got to try it. It tastes a lot better than it smells, trust me. Just one bite....

(*Terry tastes the stinky tofu and <u>grimaces</u>.*)

John: So? What do you think? Should I get us a double order?!

Terry: Well, you're right about one part—it doesn't taste as bad as it smells. But stinky tofu is still a little too <u>pungent</u> for my taste!

譯 文

談論食物與享受美食

泰瑞吃完他的香腸，但是他還覺得餓，而且還有好多食物還沒嘗試。約翰帶他到一攤臭豆腐。

約翰：沒有吃臭豆腐的話就不算逛了夜市。

泰瑞：噢，不，我就是怕這一刻。我一直被警告要小心「ㄔㄡˋㄉㄡˋㄈㄨˇ」。

約翰：很好吃的。臭豆腐可是一道本地美食。

泰瑞：但是那個味道……。

約翰：你一定要試試。吃起來比聞起來好多了，相信我。只要一口……。

（泰瑞嘗了臭豆腐後作了個鬼臉）

約翰：所以？你覺得怎樣？我應該再幫我們叫第二盤嗎 ?!

泰瑞：呃，你對了一部分——吃起來不像聞起來那麼糟。但以我的口味來說臭豆腐還是有點太刺激了！

Word List

sample [ˋsæmpl] *v.* 嘗試；試吃；試用
stinky [ˋstɪŋkɪ] *adj.* 發出臭味的
tofu [ˋtofu] *n.* 豆腐（= bean curd [ˋbin ˌkɝd] *n.*）
stand [stænd] *n.* 攤子；攤位
grimace [grɪˋmes] *v.* 因為疼痛、惱怒或不喜歡而扭曲臉孔、皺眉頭；作鬼臉
pungent [ˋpʌndʒənt] *adj.*（口味或氣味）強烈刺激的

3 Biz 加分片語 Nice-to-Know Phrases

CD II-03

3.1 調味／加料以搭配個人口味
Spicing/Garnishing to Suit One's Tastes

❶ You can garnish it....
您可以……加料。

例 You can garnish it any way you like.
您可以照任何您喜歡的方式加料。

❷ There are condiments....
……有調味料。

例 There are condiments over here.
這裡有調味料。

❸ You have a choice of....
您有很多……可以選擇。

例 You have a choice of toppings.
您有很多外層可以選擇。

❹ Is your dish salty/sweet/spicy enough?
您的菜夠鹹／甜／辣嗎？

例 Is your dish salty enough?
您的菜夠鹹嗎？

Word List

spice [spaɪs] v. 加調味料於……

garnish [`gɑrnɪʃ] v. 爲增添菜餚香色而添加裝飾配菜或調味物

condiment [`kɑndəmənt] n. 調味料；佐料

topping [`tɑpɪŋ] n. 添加在食物最上面的裝飾調味外層（如奶泡、麵包丁、調味醬等）

3.2 忌吃某物 Not Eating Something

均衡攝食非常重要，吃的好也要吃的巧，當你不吃某物時可用下列四列句來婉拒。

❶ I'm careful about....
我很小心……。
例 I'm careful about what I eat.
我對吃的東西很小心。

❷ I'm watching....
我在注意……。
例 I'm watching my waistline.
我在注意我的腰圍。

❸ I'm trying to....
我在努力……。
例 I'm trying to lose weight.
我在努力減重。

❹ I'm trying to control my (sodium/fat/carbohydrate) intake.
我在試著控制（鈉／脂肪／碳水化合物）的攝取。
例 I'm trying to control my fat intake.
我在試著控制脂肪的攝取。

Ⓦord List

waistline [ˋwestˌlaɪn] *n.* 腰圍
sodium [ˋsodɪəm] *n.* （化）鈉
fat [fæt] *n.* 脂肪；油脂
carbohydrate [ˌkɑrboˋhaɪˌdret] *n.* 碳水化合物；醣類
intake [ˋɪnˌtek] *n.* 攝取量；吸收

4 Biz 加分字彙 Nice-to-Know Vocabulary

 CD II-04

1 sliced noodles [ˋslaɪst ˋnudl̩z] *n.* 刀削麵

2 fried rice noodles [ˋfraɪd ˋraɪs ˋnudl̩z] *n.* 炒米粉

3 sesame paste noodles [ˋsɛsəmɪ ˋpest ˋnudl̩z] *n.* 麻醬麵

4 eel noodles [ˋil ˋnudl̩z] *n.* 鱔魚麵

5 oyster omelet [ˋɔɪstɚ ˋɑmlɪt] *n.* 蚵仔煎

6 Cantonese congee [͵kæntəˋniz ˋkɑndʒi] *n.* 廣東粥

7 glutinous oil rice [ˋglutɪnəs ˋɔɪl ˋraɪs] *n.* 油飯

8 boiled salted chicken [ˋbɔɪld ˋsɔltɪd ˋtʃɪkɪn] *n.* 鹽水雞

9 angelica duck [ænˋdʒɛlɪkə ˋdʌk] *n.* 當歸鴨

10 clam soup [ˋklæm ˋsup] *n.* 蛤蜊湯

11 kebab [kəˋbɑb] *n.* 烤肉串

12 shaved ice [ˋʃevd ˋaɪs] *n.* 剉冰

13 pearl milk tea [ˋpɝl ˋmɪlk ˋti] *n.* 珍珠奶茶

14 tofu pudding [ˋtofu ˋpudɪŋ] *n.* 豆花

15 cotton candy [ˋkɑtn̩ ˋkændɪ] *n.* 棉花糖

::::::::: 小心陷阱 :::::::::

☹ 錯誤用法

There are **many crowds** at the night market.

夜市非常擁擠。

☺ 正確用法

The night market is **very crowded.**

夜市非常擁擠。

::::::::: 文化小叮嚀 :::::::::

Not everyone feels comfortable in crowds. If a night market is especially busy, you should warn your guests <u>ahead of time</u> about what they are <u>getting</u> themselves <u>into</u>. Beware of <u>pickpockets</u> in crowded places, and remind guests to <u>keep</u> their wallets, handbags, and other <u>valuables</u> <u>secured</u>.

In case you and your guest become separated in a crowded place, you should arrange a place to meet up, like a <u>prominent</u> landmark, sign etc. Moreover, make sure your guest has a card with the name and address of their hotel written on it in the local language. They should also, of course, already have your name card with your <u>contact numbers</u>.

並不是每一個人都習慣置身人群當中。如果夜市剛好特別熱鬧的話，你應該事先提醒你的客人他們即將進入的地方會是什麼樣子。在擁擠的地方要當心扒手，並要提醒客人好好保管皮夾、手提袋和其他貴重物品。

為了預防你和客人在擁擠的地方走散，你們應該約好一個地方碰頭，像是一個明顯的地標、招牌看板等。此外，應確定你的客人帶有一張以當地語言寫著他們住宿飯店及地址的卡片。當然，他們應該也已經有載有你聯絡電話的名片。

Ⓦord List

ahead of time 事先

get into [ˌgɛt ˋɪntu] *phr.v.* 陷入；涉入

pickpocket [ˋpɪkˌpɑkɪt] *n.* 扒手

keep sth. secured 將某物妥善保管

valuables [ˋvæljuəblz] *n.* （通常複數）（體積不大的）貴重物品

prominent [ˋprɑmənənt] *adj.* 顯要的；明顯的

contact number [ˋkɑntækt ˌnʌmbɚ] *n.* 聯絡電話號碼

5 實戰演練 Practice Exercises

I 請為下列三題選出最適本章的中文譯義。

1 in season

(A) 經過調味的 (B) 在某季 (C) 正值旺季

2 have a weakness for...

(A) 有……的弱點 (B) 害怕…… (C) 抗拒不了……

3 siren song

(A) 警車笛聲 (B) 救護車響 (C) 致命吸引

II 你會如何回應下列這兩句話？

1 This Buffalo Chicken Wings is a little too spicy for my taste.

(A) Don't worry, you won't get fat if you keep regular workout.

(B) There are condiments over here.

(C) There is a water fountain over there. Next time maybe you should stick with the beef.

2 I must admit I have a weakness for fried food.

(A) Eating fried food at a night market is what you could call a guilty pleasure.

(B) Admitting things isn't a sign of weakness.

(C) It makes me feel weak too.

III 你和客人去逛夜市，一個小販剛好端東西出來，你的客人看見並問你那是什麼。請利用下列詞語寫出一則簡答：

stall	a local delicacy	be dipped in batter
be fried in oil	basil	garnish

＊解答請見 234 頁

第 **10** 章

語言
Language

One of the defining elements of culture is language. If you are reading this book, odds are you sometimes find yourself in a position where you have to bridge the communication gap between your culture and someone else's. Being able to talk about a language's meaning, rules, and nuances, as well as being able to discuss the similarities and differences between your respective languages can be an asset for you when socializing and doing business with foreigners.

語言是定義文化的要素之一。假如你現在在讀這本書,很有可能你會發現自己有時所處的位置必須去彌合自己文化與他人文化之間的溝通隔閡。和外國人交際、做生意時,如果能夠論述一種語言的意義、規則和細微差異,並且能討論彼此語言之間的同異處的話,對你而言會是一種有利的資產。

1 Biz 必通句型 Need-to-Know Phrases

CD II-05

1.1 口語 Spoken Language

你的客人也許不怎麼懂中文,說不定會有興趣向你學幾句簡單實用的話。下列這八句可以用來解說和串場。

---

❶ ... is a <u>tonal</u> language, with (number) <u>distinct</u> tones.
……是一種聲調語言,有(數量)個明顯不同的聲調。

例 Mandarin Chinese is a tonal language with four distinct tones.
國語是一種聲調語言,有四個明顯不同的聲調。

---

❷ (Language) grammar (is/is not) very (complicated/<u>straightforward</u>).
(語言)語法(是/不是)很(複雜/簡單)。

例 English grammar is very complicated, but Chinese grammar is quite straightforward.
英文語法很複雜,但中文語法則相當簡單。

---

❸ ... is a language of great....
……是一種富……的語言。

例 Chinese is a language of great variety; it has many regional <u>dialects</u>.
中文是一種多樣化的語言;它有許多地區方言。

Word **L**ist

tonal [`tonl] *adj.* 聲調的;音調的;色調的(聲調語言 tonal language 或 tone language,各別的字因音的高低不同而意思不同,如中文、泰語等)

distinct [dɪ`stɪŋkt] *adj.* 明顯不同的;明顯的;清楚的

straightforward [ˌstret`fɔrwɚd] *adj.* (事)簡單容易的;(人)率直的

dialect [`daɪəlɛkt] *n.* 方言

❹ Many people here are <u>fluent</u> in....

這裡有很多人……說得很流利。

例 Many people here are fluent in two or more dialects.

這裡有很多人能說兩種或更多的方言。

❺ (Somebody) is fluent in... and <u>conversant</u> in....

（某人）的……說得很流利，而且精通……。

例 Alice is fluent in French and Spanish and conversant in German.

愛麗絲的法語與西班牙語說得很流利，而且精通德語。

❻ When I was in (place), I learned a little bit of <u>survival</u> (language).

我在（地方）的時候，學了一點點的「活命」（語言）。

例 When I was in Moscow, I learned a little bit of survival Russian.

我在莫斯科的時候，學了一點點「活命」俄語。

❼ (Somebody) has a(n) (adj.)... <u>accent</u>.

（某人）有股（形容詞）……腔。

例 Steven has a strong Beijing accent.

史帝芬有股很重的北京腔。

❽ ... has a lot in common with....

……和……有很多共通處。

例 French has a lot in common with Spanish.

法語和西班牙語有很多共通處。

Ⓦ ord List

fluent [`fluənt] *adj.* 流利的；流暢的
conversant [`kɑnvɚsn̩t] *adj.* 熟悉的；精通的

survival [sɚ`vaɪvl] *n.* 存活；倖存（survival language 指基礎實用的語言，如到異國旅遊、出差前短時間內學的救急情境短句等）

accent [`æksɛnt] *n.* 腔調；口音；重音符號

1.2 文字 Written Language

即使學習中文多年的外國人也覺得辨識漢字是最困難的一部份，你的解說或許能讓外國客人對結構複雜的方塊字有些許的認識，先從筆劃開始吧。

---

❶ This <u>character</u> has (number) <u>strokes</u>.
這個字有（數量）劃。
例 This character has sixteen strokes.
這個字有 16 劃。

再來解釋部首。

---

❷ This part of (the character) is the <u>radical</u> that means....
（字）的這部分是部首，意思是⋯⋯。
例 This part of「河」is the radical that means "water."
「河」的這部分是部首，意思是「水」。

接著說明發音。

---

❸ This character is pronounced....
這個字唸作⋯⋯。
例 This character is pronounced "fēi."
這個字唸作「ㄈㄟ」。

---

ord List

character [`kærəktə] *n.* 字（漢字、英文字母等書寫符號；常指中文的方塊字）
stroke [strok] *n.* 筆劃；（寫字、繪畫的）一筆
radical [`rædɪkl] *n.*（漢字的）部首

下列這三句用來解說意思。

❹ This character means....
這個字是……的意思。
例 This character means "slow."
這個字是「慢」的意思。

❺ ... is the character for....
……這個字是指……。
例 「鳳」 is the character for "phoenix."
「鳳」這個字是指「鳳凰」。

❻ This character <u>symbolizes</u>....
這個字象徵……。
例 This character symbolizes <u>vitality</u>.
這個字象徵活力。

漢字是圖形文字，六書中的象形尤其可以看出物的本身。

❼ See how this part of (the character) looks like...?
看（字）的這部分像不像……？
例 See how this part of "語" looks like a mouth?
看「語」的這部分像不像一張嘴？

❽ Some characters have a special power, like....
有些字有特殊的力量，像……。
例 Some characters have a special power, like "fú."
有些字有特殊的力量，像「福」。

 Word List

symbolize [ˈsɪmbḷˌaɪz] *v.* 象徵；代表
vitality [vaɪˈtælətɪ] *n.* 活力；朝氣

2 實戰會話 Show Time

2.1 Spoken Language

CD II-06

John and Terry are talking, and the American has some questions about the Chinese language for his host.

Terry: I'm curious to know about Chinese, John. I've heard it's a difficult language to learn.

John: Well, I don't know if it's really harder or easier than any other. Mandarin is a tonal language, with four distinct tones.

Terry: And if I don't use the <u>proper</u> tone, I won't <u>make sense</u>, right?

John: (*Laughing*.) Basically. Either what you say won't have any meaning, or it might have a meaning different from the one you <u>intended</u>.

Terry: What about the grammar?

John: Mandarin is a language of great <u>economy</u>. We like to keep it short and <u>to the point</u>, so the grammar is very straightforward.

Terry: Unlike English! And so many Chinese people study English too.

John: Of course—it's the international language. Many people here are fluent in both languages.

譯 文

口語

約翰和泰瑞正在聊天，這位美國人有一些與中文有關的問題要問問他的東道。

泰瑞：約翰，我很好奇想瞭解一下中文。我聽說它是一種很難學的語言。

約翰：這個嘛，我不知道它到底是比別的語言更難學還是更好學。中文是一種聲調語言，有四個明顯不同的聲調。

泰瑞：所以如果我沒有用對聲調，就會不知所云，對嗎？

約翰：（笑）基本上是這樣。不是你講的話不具任何意義，就是意義可能跟你想講的不一樣。

泰瑞：語法呢？

約翰：中文是一種非常符合經濟效益的語言。我們喜歡簡潔扼要，所以語法很簡單。

泰瑞：跟英文不一樣！而且這麼多華人也在學英文。

約翰：當然──它是國際語言。這裡有很多人這兩種語言都精通。

Word List

proper [`prɑpɚ] *adj.* 適合的；恰當的
make sense 有意義；有道理
intend [ɪn`tɛnd] *v.* 意指……；打算……（intend to do sth. 打算做某事）
economy [ɪ`kɑnəmɪ] *n.* 節約；經濟；節省
to the point 扼要；中肯

2.2 Written Language

Terry is asking John about the meaning of a character on a menu in a fine restaurant.

Terry: So what is this character?

John: This character is pronounced "niú."

Terry: And it means...?

John: "牛" is the character for "cow."

Terry: How do you get cow out of that?

John: Well, think about it as a picture. See how this part of the character looks like a cow's head?

Terry: Yeah, I see what you mean. Are all characters like that?

John: No. (*Smiling.*) Unfortunately, it's not that easy.

Terry: So they're not all pictures?

John: Some characters started as pictures, while others <u>represent</u> a sound or are <u>metaphors</u>. There are six different types in all.

Terry: So how do you <u>tell the difference</u>?

John: Lots of study!

譯文

文字

在一家精緻的餐廳裡，泰瑞正在問約翰菜單上某個字的意思。

泰瑞：那這是什麼字？

約翰：這個字唸作「ㄋㄧㄡˊ」。

泰瑞：意思是⋯⋯？

約翰：「牛」這個字是指「牛」。

泰瑞：你們怎麼從這個字得出牛（*的意思*）？

約翰：呃，把它想成一幅圖畫。看字的這個部分像不像一隻牛的頭？

泰瑞：喔，我懂你的意思了。所有的字都像這樣嗎？

約翰：不是。（*微笑*）可惜，沒有那麼簡單。

泰瑞：所以不全都是圖畫囉？

約翰：有一些字是從圖畫開始的，然而其他的代表聲音或是象徵。總共有六種不同的類型。

泰瑞：那你們怎麼區分的？

約翰：一堆學問！

represent [ˌrɛprɪˋzɛnt] *v.* 代表；象徵
metaphor [ˋmɛtəfɚ] *n.* 象徵；（修辭法）隱喻
tell the difference 分辨不同；區分差異

3 Biz 加分句型 Nice-to-Know Phrases

 CD II-07

3.1 發音——解說國語的聲調
Pronunciation－Describing Mandarin's Tones

❶ The first tone is a high, <u>even</u> sound, just like "bā"
一聲是高音、平調，就像「八」。【陰平】

❷ The second tone is a high, <u>rising</u> sound, just like "bá."
二聲是高音、上升調，就像「拔」。【陽平】

❸ The third tone is a <u>falling</u> and rising sound, just like "bǎ"
三聲是先降後升調，就像「把」。【上聲】

❹ The forth tone falls from high to low (like a <u>command</u>), just like "bà."
四聲由高音降至低音（像命令），就像「爸」。【去聲】

❺ The fifth tone is known as the "<u>neutral</u>" tone, or "<u>light</u>" tone, and is short and light, just like "ba."
第五聲即所謂的「輕音」或「輕聲」，短又輕，就像「吧」。

Word List

even [ˋivən] *adj.* 平坦的；齊的；偶數的

rising [ˋraɪzɪŋ] *adj.* 上升的；上揚的

falling [ˋfɔlɪŋ] *adj.* 落下的；下降的

command [kəˋmænd] *n.* 命令；控制；掌握

neutral [ˋnjutrəl] *adj.* 淡的；中立的

light [laɪt] *adj.* 輕的；淡的；少的

3.2 談論某人的第一語言
Talking About One's <u>First Language</u>

❶ ... is/isn't (somebody's) <u>mother tongue</u>.
……是/不是（某人的）母語。
例 Spanish isn't my mother tongue; I learned it in college.
西班牙文不是我的母語，我是在大學學的。

❷ ... is/isn't (somebody's) first language.
……是/不是（某人的）第一語言。
例 French is her first language, you can ask her if you don't understand these <u>slang</u> and <u>idioms</u>.
法語是她的第一語言，如果你不懂這些俚語和慣用語的話可以問她。

❸ ... is/isn't a <u>native speaker</u> of ....
（某人）是/不是以（語言）為母語的人。
例 Yumiko isn't a native speaker of Chinese, but she can make perfect <u>retroflexion</u>.
由美子不是以中文為母語的人，但她能發漂亮的捲舌音。

❹ ... speaks... well, but he/she isn't a native speaker.
……很會說……，但他／她不是個母語人士。
例 Bruno speaks Korean well, but he isn't a native speaker.
布魯諾很會說韓國話，但他不是個母語人士。

Word List

first language [ˈfɝst ˈlæŋgwɪdʒ] 第一語言（一個人所學會的第一種語言，或是一個地區、社會裡最多人說的語言）

mother tongue [ˈmʌðɚ ˈtʌŋ] 母語 (=native tongue, native language)

slang [slæŋ] n.（不可數）俚語（不適於較正式的場合，有些只有特定族群在用）

idiom [ˈɪdɪəm] n. 慣用語；成語；歇後語

native speaker [ˈnetɪv ˈspikɚ] 以某種語言為母語的人

retroflexion [ˌrɛtrəˈflɛkʃən] n. 捲舌音

4 Biz 加分字彙 Nice-to-Know Vocabulary

 CD II-08

❶ **Hanyu Pinyin** 漢語拼音

❷ **articulate** [ɑr`tɪkjəlɪt] *adj.* 發音清晰的；善於表達的

❸ **vernacular** [vɚ`nækjələ-] *n.* 方言；本地話

❹ **Hakka** [`hɑk`kɑ] *n.* 客家話；客家人

❺ **aborigine** [æbə`rɪdʒəni] *n.* 原住民

❻ **oracle bone script** [`ɔrəkl̩ `bon `skrɪpt] *n.* 甲骨文

❼ **seal script** [`sil `skrɪpt] *n.* 篆書

❽ **clerical script** [`klɛrɪkl̩ `skrɪpt] *n.* 隸書

❾ **standard script** [`stændɚd `skrɪpt] *n.* 楷書

❿ **semi-cursive script** [ˌsɛmɪ`kɚsɪv `skrɪpt] *n.* 行書

⓫ **cursive script** [`kɚsɪv `skrɪpt] *n.* 草書

⓬ **pictograph** [`pɪktəˌgræf] *n.* 象形字

⓭ **indicative** [ɪn`dɪkətɪv] *n.* 指事字

⓮ **ideograph** [`ɪdɪə`græf] *n.* 會意字

⓯ **semantic-phonetic compound** [sə`mæntɪk fo`nɛtɪk `kɑmpaʊnd]
   n. 形聲字

::::::::: 小心陷阱 :::::::::

☹ 錯誤用法

Spanish is my **mother's tongue**.
西班牙是我的母語。

☺ 正確用法

Spanish is my **mother tongue**.
西班牙話是我的母語。

::::::::: 文化小叮嚀 :::::::::

One of the biggest <u>obstacles</u> <u>facing</u> people who are learning a new language is a lack of <u>confidence</u>. If your guest is trying to speak your language, <u>encourage</u> him or her and <u>compliment</u> them often when they express themselves clearly and correctly. One of the biggest <u>frustrations</u> facing foreigners who are learning to speak a tonal language (like Mandarin) is the <u>phenomenon</u> <u>linguists</u> refer to as "lock-up." This phrase has been <u>coined</u> to describe the situation where a native speaker of a language is unable to understand a non-native speaker, despite their correct pronunciation and use of tones, because of the fact that the person talking does not "look like" a native speaker. Some non-Asians **can**, and **do**, speak Asian languages fluently, so don't be surprised when you meet them.

正在學一種新語言的人常面對的最大障礙之一就是缺乏自信。如果你的客人試著說你的語言，應該鼓勵他或她，並在他們清楚且正確表達自己時多給予讚美。
正在學說一種聲調語言（如中文）的外國人常遭遇的最大挫折之一就是語言學家所謂的「上鎖」現象。這個詞 (lock-up) 被創造來描述這樣的現象：當以某語言為母語的人聽不懂非母語人士所說的話，儘管他們的發音及聲調皆正確無誤，只因為說話者「看起來」不像母語人士。有一些非亞洲人**能**，也**的確**，說一口流利的亞洲語言，所以遇見他們的時候不要太驚訝。

Ｗord List

obstacle [`ɑbstək] *n.* 阻力；障礙
face [fes] *v.* 面對；正視；面臨
confidence [`kɑnfədəns] *n.* 信心；自信
encourage [ɪn`kɝɪdʒ] *v.* 鼓勵；鼓舞
compliment [`kɑmpləmənt] *v./n.* 稱讚；恭維

frustration [ˌfrʌs`treʃən] *n.* 挫折
phenomenon [fə`nɑməˌnɑn] *n.* 現象；景象
linguist [`lɪŋgwɪst] *n.* 語言學家
lock-up [`lɑk ˌʌp] *n.* 上鎖現象（為語言學專用術語）
coin [kɔɪn] *v.* 創造、發明新詞

5 實戰演練 Practice Exercises

I 請為下列三題選出最適本章的中文譯義。

1 distinct tones

(A) 明顯不同的色調　(B) 有所區別的聲調　(C) 清楚明白的語氣

2 have a lot in common

(A) 共同擁有許多財富　(B) 擁有很多常見的事物　(C) 有許多共通之處

3 short and to the point

(A) 直擊要害　(B) 短而尖銳　(C) 簡潔扼要

II 你會如何回應下面這兩句話？

1 When I was in Moscow, I learned a little bit of survival Russian.

(A) That's very impressive. Is it a difficult language?

(B) I've always been curious to know how the Russians learned to survive.

(C) Wow! So you're already fluent!

2 What's your mother tongue?

(A) My mother speaks Taiwanese and Mandarin.

(B) I grew up speaking Taiwanese at home.

(C) What did you say about my mother's tongue?

III 你的客人問你一個字的意思，你不僅回答，並且解說字的發音、聲調和筆劃數等。請利用下列詞語寫出一則簡短的解說：

character	be pronounced	tone	mean
this part	look like	strokes	

＊解答請見 235 頁

廟宇
Temples

Temples are often colorful and fascinating places, especially for foreign visitors who might be seeing a Buddhist or Taoist temple up close for the first time. It's natural for them to be curious, and your explanations can take some of the mystery out of what they're seeing. You'll be giving your guests a glimpse into your culture's religious beliefs and practices that they'll likely remember for a lifetime.

廟宇通常是色彩鮮豔、引人入勝的地方，尤其對也許是第一次近看佛教或道教廟宇的外國訪客而言。他們好奇是正常的，你的解說能幫忙褪去他們所見事物的一些神秘色彩。你將引領你的客人一窺你文化宗教信仰和敬神方式，這可能是他們永生難忘的經驗。

1 Biz 必通句型 Need-to-Know Phrases

 CD II-09

1.1 談論廟宇 Talking About a <u>Temple</u>

❶ **This is a... temple. <u>It's dedicated to</u> the god/<u>goddess</u> (name).**

這是一座……廟宇，供奉的是（名稱）神／女神。

例 This is a <u>Taoist</u> temple. It's dedicated to the goddess Matsu.

這是一座道教的廟宇，供奉的是媽祖娘娘。

❷ **... is the god/goddess of....**

（神／女神名）是……神。

例 Matsu is the goddess of the sea.

媽祖是女海神。

❸ **As you can see, the temple <u>architecture</u> is (adj.).**

如您所見，廟宇的建築是（形容詞）。

例 As you can see, the temple architecture is <u>typically</u> colorful and <u>ornate</u>.

如您所見，廟宇的建築多半是色彩鮮豔、裝飾華麗。

Word List

temple [`tɛmpl̩] *n.* 廟宇（佛教廟宇統稱 "寺院" ；道教廟宇統稱 "宮觀"）

be dedicated to sth. 奉獻給某事物；獻身致力於某事物

goddess [`gɑdɪs] *n.* 女神

Taoist [`tauɪst] *adj.* 道教（徒）的；道家的；*n.* 道教徒

architecture [`ɑrkə͵tɛktʃɚ] *n.* 建築風格、設計；建築物

typically [`tɪpɪklɪ] *adv.* 典型地；向來

ornate [ɔr`net] *adj.* 裝飾華麗的

❹ This temple has been rebuilt (number) <u>times</u>.
這座廟被重建了（數目）次。
例 This temple has been rebuilt three times.
這座廟被重建了三次。

❺ The original temple was built (location) in (year).
原來的廟在（年份）建於（位置）。
例 The original temple was built on this site in 1928.
原來的廟在 1928 年建於這個地點。

❻ Every year, this temple is (the site of/the place where) (event takes place).
每年，這座廟都是（活動舉行）的（地點／地方）。
例 Every year, this temple is the site where a large <u>pilgrimage</u> <u>starts out</u>.
每年，這座廟都是一個大規模進香活動出發的地點。

❼ The (<u>symbol/image/icon</u> etc.) represents....
這個（符號／圖像／畫像等）代表⋯⋯。
例 The image of the dragon represents power.
這個龍的圖像代表權力。

❽ <u>Devotees</u> of... believe....
⋯⋯的信徒相信⋯⋯。
例 Devotees of Guan Gong believe he was once a powerful <u>general</u> who <u>went on</u> to become a god.
關公的信徒相信他曾經是一位威鎮八方的將軍，後來才昇化成神。

Ⓦord List

time [taɪm] *n.* （可數）次數；倍
pilgrimage [ˋpɪlgrəmɪdʒ] *n.* 進香；朝聖
start out [ˋstɑrt ˋaʊt] *phr. v.* 啓程；出發
symbol [ˋsɪmbl] *n.* 符號；標誌；記號
image [ˋɪmɪdʒ] *n.* 雕像；塑像；圖像

icon [ˋaɪkɑn] *n.* 神像；塑像；塑像
devotee [ˌdɛvəˋti] *n.* 宗教信徒；熱衷致力者
general [ˋdʒɛnərəl] *n.* 將軍；將官
go on [ˋgo ˌɑn] *phr. v.* 接著⋯⋯；繼續⋯⋯

1.2 典禮、拜神和儀式 <u>Ceremonies</u>, <u>Devotions</u>, and <u>Rituals</u>

下列這五句可以用來向客人解說常見的宗教典禮和儀式。

❶ This <u>parade</u> <u>commemorates</u> (event).
這場繞境是在紀念（事件）。
例 This parade commemorates Matsu's birthday.
這場繞境是在紀念媽祖誕辰。【為農曆 3 月 23 日】

❷ People come to the temple to ask the god....
民眾來廟裡請求神明⋯⋯。
例 People come to the temple to ask the god for <u>guidance</u> when making big decisions.
做重要決定時，民眾會來廟裡請求神明指示。

❸ These people are making <u>offerings</u> to....
這些人在祭供，為的是⋯⋯。
例 These people are making offerings to ask the goddess for help in <u>conceiving</u> a child.
這些人在祭供，為的是請娘娘庇佑得子。

❹ The purpose of this <u>ritual/ceremony</u> is....
這個儀式／典禮的目的是⋯⋯。
例 The purpose of this ritual is to <u>drive away</u> <u>evil spirits</u>.
這個儀式的目的是去邪。

Ⓦord List

ceremony [`sɛrə,monɪ] *n.* 典禮；儀式
devotions [dɪ`voʃənz] *n.* （複數形）祈禱；拜神
ritual [`rɪtʃʊəl] *n.* 儀式
parade [pə`red] *n.* 行進隊伍；遊行
commemorate [kə`mɛmə,ret] *v.* 紀念；慶祝

guidance [`gaɪdn̩s] *n.* 建議；指示
offering [`ɔfərɪŋ] *n.* 祭物；香油錢；提供（物）
conceive [kən`siv] *v.* 懷胎
drive away *phr. v.* 驅離；使⋯⋯遠離
evil spirit [`ivl̩ `spɪrɪt] *n.* 惡靈；邪物

❺ ... has/have a <u>ceremonial</u> function.

……具有儀式上的功用。

例 The weapons the <u>shaman</u> is using have a ceremonial function.

道士在使用的兵器具有儀式上的功用。

廟裡常見刻文，你的客人應該會非常高興聽你翻譯。

❻ The <u>inscription</u> reads....

刻文說：……。

例 The inscription reads: God bless human beings.

刻文說：神佑黎民。

❼ The belief that... is a central <u>tenet</u> of (religion).

……的信念是（宗教）的主要教義。

例 The belief that people will be <u>reincarnated</u> is a central tenet of <u>Buddhism</u>.

相信人會轉世是佛教的的主要教義。

❽ About (percentage) of (country)'s population is....

（國家）的人口約有（比率）是……。

例 About two percent of Taiwan's population is <u>Christian</u>.

台灣約有 2% 的人口是基督徒。

Ⓦord List

ceremonial [ˌsɛrəˈmonɪəl] *adj.* （用於）典禮的

shaman [ˈʃɑmən] *n.* 能通靈治病的道士；巫師

inscription [ɪnˈskrɪpʃən] *n.* 刻寫的文字

tenet [ˈtɛnɪt] *n.* 教義；信條

reincarnate [ˌrimˈkɑrˌnet] *v.* 轉世再生

Buddhism [ˈbudɪzəm] *n.* 佛教

Christian [ˈkrɪstʃən] *n.* 基督教徒；*adj.* 基督教（徒）的

2 實戰會話 Show Time

CD II-10

2.1 A Prayer

While passing a temple, Terry expressed interest and asked John <u>a number of</u> questions. John has offered to take him into the temple for a look around.

John: This is a typical <u>neighborhood</u> temple.

Terry: What religion might these people be?

John: They're Taoists. This is a Taoist temple. It's dedicated to the god Tu Di Gong.

Terry: Tu Di Gong?

John: Yes. Tu Di Gong is the god of the land.

Terry: What are they doing over there?

John: Those people are making offerings to ask Tu Di Gong to protect this area. People also come to the temple to ask the god questions about what they should and shouldn't do in their daily lives.

Terry: <u>Fascinating</u>.

祈福

經過一座廟的時候，泰瑞表示興趣並問了約翰一些問題。約翰提議帶他進廟裡看一下。

約翰：這是一座典型的地方廟宇。

泰瑞：這些人信的是什麼教？

約翰：他們是道教徒。這是一座道教的宮觀，供奉的是土地公。

泰瑞：土地公？

約翰：對。土地公是土地神。

泰瑞：他們在那裡做什麼？

約翰：這些人在祭供，為的是請土地公保護這個地區。民眾也來廟裡請求神明指示日常生活中的宜、忌問題。

泰瑞：真有趣。

....
a number of 一些；數個
neighborhood [`nebɚ͵hud] *n.* 鄰近地區；四鄰；街坊
fascinating [`fæsn͵etɪŋ] *adj.* 令人覺得有趣的；令人感興趣的

2.2 A Temple History

Terry and John are standing outside another temple, this one much larger and more famous than the first. John has just finished reading a <u>plaque</u> and is <u>relating</u> the information to his guest.

John: The plaque gives a history of Lungshan Temple. It says that the temple has been rebuilt several times. The original temple was built on this site in 1738. The temple we see only <u>dates back to</u> the late 1990's.

Terry: What happened to the other temples?

John: Let's see... an earthquake in 1814, a typhoon in 1867, been eaten by <u>termites</u>, American bombs in 1945....

Terry: <u>Yikes</u>.

John: As you can see, the temple architecture is typical of a Taoist temple. Look at all the <u>figures</u> on the roof.

Terry: It's beautiful. And what an amazing story!

譯 文

廟的歷史

泰瑞和約翰站在另一座廟外，這座廟比第一座大了許多，也更有名。約翰剛讀完一面石牌，正在向他的客人講述上面的資訊。

約翰：牌上講的是龍山寺的歷史。它說這座廟被重建了很多次，原來的廟在 1738 年建於這個地點。我們現在看到的廟是 1990 年代末期蓋的。

泰瑞：其他的廟發生了什麼事？

約翰：我們來看一下……，1814 年一場地震，1867 年一個颱風，遭白蟻侵蝕，1945 年美軍轟炸……。

泰瑞：唉呀。

約翰：如您所見，這座廟的建築是典型的道教宮觀。你看屋頂上那些雕飾。

泰瑞：好美，而且故事非常精彩！

Word List

plaque [plæk] *n.* 匾；牌；飾板
relate [rɪ`let] *v.* 敘述；講
date back to.... 起始於……；追溯至……
the late 1990's 1990 年代晚期
termite [`tɝmaɪt] *n.* 白蟻
yikes [jaɪks] 哎呀（驚嚇或害怕時發出的感嘆詞）
figure [`fɪgjɚ] *n.* 雕塑；人像；圖像

3 Biz 加分句型 Nice-to-Know Phrases

CD II-11

3.1 廟宇規矩 Temple <u>Etiquette</u>

❶ **We'<u>re</u> not really <u>dressed</u> <u>appropriately</u> to....**
我們的衣著不太適合⋯⋯。
例 We're not really dressed appropriately to go inside──we should come back another time.
我們的衣著不太適合進去──我們應該下次再來。

❷ **That's a private temple. We should....**
那是一座私人廟宇,我們應該⋯⋯。
例 That's a private temple. We should ask <u>permission</u> before we go in.
那是一座私人廟宇,我們進去之前應該先徵得同意。

❸ **We <u>had better</u> enter....**
我們最好從⋯⋯進入
例 We had better enter through one of the side doors.
我們最好從其中一個側門進入。

❹ **Don't forget to....**
不要忘了⋯⋯。
例 Don't forget to take off your shoes at the door.
不要忘記在門口將鞋子脫下。

ord List

etiquette [ˋɛtɪkɛt] *n.* 禮儀;規矩
be dressed 身著衣物
appropriately [əˋproprɪ͵etlɪ] *adv.* 適當地

permission [pɚˋmɪʃən] *n.* 許可;准許
had better V. 最好⋯⋯

3.2 談論和尚與尼姑 Talking About Monks and Nuns

❶ There's a monastery/nunnery....
……有僧院／尼姑庵。

例 There's a nunnery attached to the temple.
廟的旁邊有一座尼姑庵。

❷ The monks spend a large amount of time....
和尚們花很多時間……。

例 The monks spend a large amount of time meditating and studying scriptures every day.
和尚每天花很多時間打坐誦經。

❸ The monks still....
和尚們依舊……。

例 The monks still beg alms, as they have for thousands of years.
和尚依舊化緣，就跟他們幾千年來一樣。

❹ All the monks here....
這裡所有的和尚都……。

例 All the monks here are vegetarians; they think eating meat and fish is bad for karma.
這裡所有的和尚都吃素，他們認為吃肉和魚對業報不好。

Word List

monk [mʌŋk] *n.* （佛教）和尚；（天主教、東正教）修士

nun [nʌn] *n.* （佛教）尼姑；（天主教、東正教）修女

monastery [`mɑnəsˌtɛrɪ] *n.* 僧院；修道院

nunnery [`nʌnərɪ] *n.* 尼姑庵；女修道院

attached [ə`tætʃt] *adj.* 黏附的；附屬的

a large amount of 大量的……

meditate [`mɛdəˌtet] *v.* 冥想；沉思

scripure [`skrɪptʃɚ] *n.* 宗教的聖書經文（the Scripture 指聖經）

alms [ɑmz] *n.* 施捨（物）；救濟（品）

vegetarian [ˌvɛdʒə`tɛrɪən] *n.* 素食者；*adj.* 素食（者）的

karma [`kɑrmə] *n.* （佛家語）業；業報（業為人在世的所有活動作為，將決定六道生死輪迴）

4 Biz 加分字彙 Nice-to-Know Vocabulary

 CD II-12

1 **Confucianism** [kən`fjuʃə͵nɪzm̩] *n.* 儒家；孔子學說

2 **polytheistic** [pɑlɪθi`ɪstɪk] *adj.* 多神崇拜的

3 **deity** [`diətɪ] *n.* 神

4 **altar** [`ɔltɚ] *n.* 神壇；聖壇

5 **incense** [`ɪnsɛns] *n.* 香， incense stick [`ɪnsɛns `stɪk] *n.* 香支

6 **ghost money** [`gost `mʌnɪ]; **spirit money** [`spɪrɪt `mʌnɪ] *n.* 紙錢

7 **spirit medium** [`spɪrɪt `midɪəm] *n.* 靈媒

8 **fortune-teller** [`fɔrtʃən ͵tɛlɚ] *n.* 算命仙；算命師

9 **palanquin** [͵pælən`kin] *n.* 轎子

10 **ancestor** [`ænsɛstɚ] *n.* 祖先

11 **descendant** [dɪ`sɛndənt] *n.* 子孫；後代

12 **mural** [`mjʊrəl] *n.* 壁畫

13 **the Jade Emperor** [ðə `dʒed `ɛmpərɚ] *n.* 玉皇大帝

14 **the Eight Immortals** [ðə `et ɪ`mɔrtl̩z] *n.* 八仙

15 **charm** [tʃɑrm] *n.* 符咒；咒語；護身符
　　amulet [`æmjəlɪt] *n.* 護身符；避邪物

::::::: 小心陷阱 :::::::

☹ 錯誤用法

The temple **construction** is splendid.

這座廟的建築美輪美奐。

☺ 正確用法

The temple **architecture** is splendid.

這座廟的建築美侖美奐。

::::::: 文化小叮嚀 :::::::

When foreign guests come to town, they may wish to attend worship services at a church, synagogue, or mosque, as required by their religion. It pays to be prepared with a list of the addresses and phone numbers of houses of worship in your area.

外國客人來訪時，因各別的宗教需要，他們也許會希望參加基督教堂、猶太教堂或清真寺的禮拜儀式。列出一張記有你所在地各禮拜堂的地址及電話號碼的清單備查是值得的。

ord List

worship [`wɝʃɪp] *n.* 拜（神）；崇拜；做禮拜

service [`sɝvɪs] *n.* 禮拜；宗教儀式

synagogue [`sɪnəgɔg] *n.* 猶太教會堂

mosque [mɑsk] *n.* 回教清真寺

5 實戰演練 Practice Exercises

I 請為下列三題選出最適本章的中文譯義。

❶ make offerings

(A) 做慈善 (B) 提供 (C) 祭貢

❷ date back to...

(A) 追溯至…… (B) 回憶起…… (C)回想到……

❸ beg alms

(A) 行乞 (B) 化緣 (C) 求援

II 你會如何回應下面這兩句話？

❶ This parade commemorates Matsu's birthday.

(A) I can't wait to see those energetic cheerleaders!

(B) She must be someone important and wealthy.

(C) Can we stop for a few minutes? I want to know what it's like.

❷ Are we dressed appropriately to go inside?

(A) Yes, but you should remove your hat first.

(B) Why would we wear dresses?

(C) I like your outfit.

III 你帶三位客人參觀一座佛寺，他們問你幾個有關一幅彩色壁畫的問題。請利用下列詞語寫出一則簡答：

commemorate	Buddha	the belief
is a central tenet of	represent	

＊解答請見 236 頁

第 **12**. 章

高爾夫球場
The Golf Course

Some of the biggest deals ever concluded never see the inside of a corporate boardroom—they are made with a handshake on the golf course. Indeed, golf and business seem to go hand in hand. If your foreign guest is a golfer, treating them to a round (or even a trip to the driving range) can make for an enjoyable and memorable part of their visit. The golf course also offers a golden opportunity to talk shop and do business.

有些成功的最大型買賣並非在公司的會議室內談成,而是在高爾夫球場上握手敲定的。的確,高爾夫和商務似乎是魚水關係。如果你的外國訪客是個高爾夫球手,請他們打一場球(甚或走一趟練習場)將成為他們行程中一段愉快又難忘的時光。高爾夫球場也提供了談論公事和進行交易的絕佳機會。

1 Biz 必通句型 Need-to-Know Phrases

CD II-13

1.1 談論高爾夫 Talking Golf

帶客人去打高爾夫球，應該要幫忙他們熟悉環境。

❶ **This is a (number)-hole <u>course</u>.**
這是個（洞數）洞的球場。
例 This is a nine-hole course.
'這是個九洞的球場。

❷ **Our <u>tee-off</u> time is....**
我們的開球時間是……。
例 Our tee-off time is eleven o'clock.
我們的開球時間是十一點。

❸ **I'm a (number) <u>handicap</u>, myself.**
我本身差點是（數目）。
例 I'm a fifteen handicap, myself.
我本身差點是十五。

如果忘記帶任何基本用具，大概都能在高爾夫球用品專賣店裡找到需要的東西。

Word List

course [kors] *n.* 高爾夫球場（除了 9 洞，另有 18、27 和 36 洞的高爾夫球場）
tee-off [ˌti `ɔf] *adj./n.* 高爾夫球起桿發球（tee 為插在土裡置放高爾夫球的球座）
handicap [`hændɪˌkæp] *n.* 差點（用來評估業餘高球手的球技，差點愈低，球技愈高。差點制度將球技較差的球手桿數減掉一些，使得不同程度的球手得以齊頭競賽）

❹ The <u>pro shop</u> (offers service X/sells or rents item Y.)
用品專賣店（提供某服務／有賣或出租某物）。
例 The pro shop sells <u>sunscreen</u>.
這家用品專賣店有賣防曬乳。

❺ Do you prefer to (do A) or (do B)?
您比較想（做A）還是（做B）？
例 Do you prefer to walk or rent a <u>cart</u>?
您比較想走路還是租輛球車？

❻ Do you think we ought to (do A) or (do B)?
您覺得我們應該（做A）還是（做B）？
例 Do you think we ought to play nine holes or play eighteen?
您覺得我們應該打九洞還是打十八洞？

即使你打得不錯，對自己的球技還是謙虛一點比較好。

❼ (Somebody) needs to work on (golf skill).
（某人）還需要加強（高爾夫技巧）。
例 I need to work on my <u>swing</u>.
我還需要加強我的揮桿。

❽ This is a (public/private) course.
這是個（公共的/私人的）球場。
例 This is a private course.
這是個私人的球場。

ord List

pro shop [ˋpro ˏʃɑp] *n.* 用品專賣店
sunscreen [ˋsʌnˏskrin] *n.* 防曬乳

cart [kɑrt] *n.* 高爾夫球車；購物手推車
swing [swɪŋ] *n.* 揮桿；鞦韆

1.2 開賽 Playing the Game

客人打出好球，給予讚美準沒錯。

❶ Nice (<u>putt</u>, <u>drive</u>, <u>shot</u>, etc.),...!
（推、開、打等）得漂亮，……！
例 Nice putt, Richard!
推得漂亮，理察！

❷ I <u>hooked</u> that one (direction).
我把那球拐向（方向）去了。
例 I hooked that one left.
我把那球拐太左邊了。

❸ That's a (number)-<u>stroke</u> <u>penalty</u>.
那要罰（桿數）桿。
例 That's a two-stroke penalty.
那要罰兩桿。

❹ Watch out for that (<u>hazard</u>) (location).
小心（地方）的那個（障礙）。
例 Watch out for that <u>sand trap</u> to the right of the <u>green</u>.
"小心果嶺右側的那個沙坑。

Ⓦord List

putt [pʌt] n./v. 推桿（通常用 putter [`pʌtɚ] n.推桿打，球不離地）
drive [draɪv] n./v. 發球（通常用 driver [`draɪvɚ] n.發球桿/1號木桿打）
shot [ʃɑt] n. 一擊；一記
hook [huk] v. 擊出曲球；n. 過分偏左的左曲球
stroke [strok] n./v. 一桿；一擊
penalty [`pɛnḷtɪ] n. 犯規處罰
hazard [`hæzɚd] n. （高爾夫球的）障礙區；危險
sand trap [`sænd ˌtræp] n. 沙坑（同 bunker [`bʌŋkɚ]）
green [grin] n. 果嶺（或稱 putting green，即球洞所在的區域，此區中球只能滾動）

❺ The <u>pin</u> is (location) of the green.

旗桿在果嶺的（地方）。

例 The pin is near the right <u>edge</u> of the green.

旗桿靠近果嶺的右側邊緣。

❻ The green <u>slopes</u> (direction).

果嶺往（方向）傾斜。

例 The green slopes up and to the left.

果嶺往左上方傾斜。

❼ I'd (use/go with) a (club) in this situation.

在這種情況下，我會（用／選用）（球桿）。

例 I'd use a <u>seven-iron</u> in this situation.

在這種情況下，我會用7號鐵桿。

❽ This hole is a (long/short) <u>par</u> (number of strokes for par).

這洞是標準桿（桿數）的（長／短）洞。

例 This hole is a long par five.

這洞是標準桿五桿的長洞。

ord List

pin [pɪn] *n.* 旗桿（用以標示球洞位置）

edge [ɛdʒ] *n.* 果嶺邊緣

slope [slop] *v.* 傾斜；*n.* 坡面

seven-iron [`sɛvn̩ `aɪɚn] *n.* 7 號鐵桿（打球時一套球桿以 14 支為限，鐵桿號碼一般由 3 至 9 號；球桿號碼表示桿面角度，號碼愈小，桿面傾角愈小，擊出的球愈低愈遠）

par [pɑr] *n.* 完成一個球洞或全部球洞的標準桿數

2 實戰會話 Show Time

CD II-14

2.1 Talking Golf

John and Terry have decided to spend an afternoon on the <u>*links*</u>. *Terry brought his clubs on the trip especially for the* <u>*occasion*</u>.

Terry: It's going to be great to get out on the golf course!

John: You bet! This is an eighteen-hole course. Do you think we ought to rent a cart or walk?

Terry: Let's walk—I could use the exercise. But I didn't bring a hat. I should definitely buy one. It's a sunny day.

John: The pro shop sells hats. We can <u>pick</u> one <u>up</u> there.

Terry: Have we got enough time?

John: Lots of time—don't worry. Our tee-off time is ten o'clock.

談論高爾夫

約翰和泰瑞決定到高爾夫球場度一個下午。泰瑞這趟行程還特地帶了他的球具來，為的就是打場球。

泰瑞：待會兒到高爾夫球場上去一定會很棒！

約翰：沒錯！這是個十八洞的球場。您覺得我們應該租輛球車還是走路？

泰瑞：走路好了——我需要運動運動。但我沒帶帽子，我應該買一頂。今天是個大晴天。

約翰：用品專賣店有賣帽子，我們可以到那裡帶一頂。

泰瑞：我們時間夠嗎？

約翰：時間多得很——別擔心。我們的開球時間是十點。

Word List

links [lɪŋks] *n.* （複數形）濱海高爾夫球場（或稱為 seaside links，最原始的一種高爾夫球場地，主要的困難在不平整的球道、深草區、沙坑及地形風）

occasion [əˋkeʒən] *n.* 場合；機會

pick up [ˋpɪk ˏʌp] *phr. v.* 撿起；接（人）；學會；選購

2.2 Playing the Game

Terry and John are <u>strolling</u> the links and enjoying the fresh air, the afternoon sun, and the friendly <u>competition</u>.

John: Nice drive, Terry!

Terry: Yeah, not bad... right down the middle of the <u>fairway</u>.

John: I'm <u>up</u>. (*He prepares to hit his drive.*)

Terry: Watch out for that <u>water hazard</u> on the right.

John: I see it. (*He hits his drive.*) Oh no! I hooked that one hard right! Aaah! I'm in the water! That's a two-stroke penalty.

Terry: I hope I didn't <u>jinx</u> you....

John: Not at all. I need to work on my drive.

譯文

開賽

約翰和泰瑞漫步在球場上，享受著新鮮的空氣、午後的陽光和兩人的友誼賽。

約翰：開得漂亮，泰瑞！

泰瑞：是啊，還不錯……正好在球道的中央。

約翰：該我了。（*他準備開球*）

泰瑞：小心右邊的那個障礙水池。

約翰：我看到了。（*他擊出球*）哦，不會吧！我把那球拐得太靠右邊了。呃
　　　啊！我落水了！那要罰兩桿。

泰瑞：希望我沒有帶衰你……。

約翰：沒這回事。我需要加強我的開球。

Word List

stroll [strol] *v./n.* 漫步
competition [ˌkɑmpəˋtɪʃən] *n.* 比賽；競爭
fairway [ˋfɛrˌwe] *n.* 球道（每洞發球區 tee/teeing ground 與果嶺之間的平坦球道）
up [ʌp] *adj.* 輪到出場的
water hazard [ˋwɔtɚ ˌhæzɚd] *n.* 水障礙；障礙水池
jinx [dʒɪŋks] *v.* 使倒楣；*n.* 不祥之物

3 Biz 加分句型 Nice-to-Know Phrases

CD II-15

3.1 第十九洞（酒吧）The Nineteenth Hole

❶ I don't know about you, but I....
我不知道你怎樣，不過我……。
例 I don't know about you, but I'm <u>looking forward to</u> spending some time at the nineteenth hole.
我不知道你怎樣，不過我期待到第十九洞（酒吧）坐一下。

❷ Do you <u>fancy</u>...?
您想不想……？
例 Do you fancy a drink in the <u>clubhouse</u>?
您想不想到會館喝一杯？

❸ Time for....
是……的時候了。
例 Time for my favorite hole—the watering hole.
該是到我最喜歡的一洞——酒吧的時候了。

❹ How about having...?
……怎麼樣？
例 How about having one more round before we <u>call it a night</u>?
在我們今晚結束前，再來一回怎麼樣？

Word List

the nineteenth hole（口語）第 19 洞（高爾夫球一回合 18 洞，第 19 洞指會館中的酒吧）
look forward to N./V-ing 期待……；盼望……

fancy [`fænsɪ] v. 想要；想做
clubhouse [`klʌb͵haʊs] n. 高爾夫球會館
call it a night/day 今晚／今天就此結束

3.2 超前／計分 <u>Playing Through</u>/<u>Scoring</u>

❶ Let's let these guys play through.（當後面那組人因爲你們
而無法往前打時）
我們讓這些人超前先打吧。
例 Let's let these guys play through—they're a lot faster than us.
我們讓這些人超前先打吧，他們打得比我們快多了。

高爾夫球是講究禮儀的運動，要超前別忘了徵求先行球友的同意。

**❷ Let's ask these guys if they'd mind if we play
through.**（當你們打得比較快時）
我們來問問這些人，看他們介不介意我們超前先打。

❸ That's (<u>eagle</u>, <u>birdie</u>, etc.).
那是（老鷹、博蒂等）。
例 That's birdie.
那是博蒂。

❹ That's a (number)-shot penalty for....
……要罰（桿數）桿。
例 That's a two-shot penalty for playing <u>out of bounds</u>.
把球打出界要罰兩桿。

Ⓦord List

play through [`ple ˌθru] v. 讓……先打
score [skor] v. 得分, 計分；n. 分數, 比分
eagle [`igl] n. 老鷹（高爾夫球術語，指低於標準桿兩桿）
birdie [`bɝdɪ] n. 博蒂（高爾夫球術語，指低於標準桿一桿，戲稱"抓小鳥"）
out of bounds [ˌautəv `baundz] adv. 界外地；adj. 出界的（常縮寫成O.B.）

4 Biz 加分字彙 Nice-to-Know Vocabulary

CD II-16

1 double eagle [`dʌb!̩ `ig!̩] *n.* 雙鷹（低於標準桿三桿）

2 eagle [`ig!̩] *n.* 老鷹（低於標準桿兩桿）

3 birdie [`bɝdɪ] *n.* 博蒂（低於標準桿一桿）

4 par [pɑr] *n.* 標準桿

5 bogey [`bogɪ] *n.* 柏忌（高於標準桿一桿）

6 double bogey [`dʌb!̩ `bogɪ] *n.* 雙柏忌（高於標準桿兩桿）

7 triple bogey [`trɪp!̩ `bogɪ] *n.* 高於標準桿三桿

8 quadruple bogey [`kwɑdrup!̩ `bogɪ] *n.* 高於標準桿四桿

9 hole in one [ˌhol ɪn `wʌn] *n.* 一桿進洞（亦稱 ace [es] *n.*）

10 slice [slaɪs] *n.* 右曲球

11 sky [skaɪ] *v.* 擊、踢出高飛球（飛過高但不夠遠的球）

12 cup [kʌp] *n.* 球洞

13 caddie [`kædɪ] *n.* 桿弟；高爾夫球球僮

14 tie [taɪ] *v.* 平手, 打平；*n.* 平手, 同分

15 play off [`ple ˌɔf] *v.* 延長賽；playoff *n.* 延長賽；最後決賽階段

小心陷阱

☹ 錯誤用法

Let's rent a **car**.

我們租輛球車吧。

☺ 正確用法

Let's rent a **cart**.

我們租輛球車吧。

文化小叮嚀

Golf is one of the safest sports around. Indeed, the only real dangers facing golfers come from the weather. Sometimes your guests may not have brought sunscreen, and as a good host, you should <u>think ahead</u> and make sure to have some on hand. <u>SPF</u> 30 is generally considered strong enough to provide <u>adequate</u> protection from the sun's harmful <u>rays</u>. Sunscreen, along with a hat, is <u>essential</u> on hot days, even if skies aren't sunny.

<u>Lightning</u> is the other possible golf course danger. Always keep an eye on the weather so you don't <u>get caught</u> out <u>in</u> a <u>thunderstorm</u>.

Have fun, and play safe!

高爾夫是當今最安全的運動之一。的確，高爾夫球手所面臨的僅有真正危險來自天氣。有時候你的客人也許沒有帶防曬乳液，身為一個盡職的東道，你應該預先設想，確定手邊有幾瓶可供使用。防曬係數30一般認為足以提供適當的保護抵擋陽光中的有害射線。防曬乳液，加上一頂帽子，在大熱天是必備的，即使天上的陽光不強。

閃電是另一個在高爾夫球場上可能會碰到的危險。隨時注意天氣，這樣你才不會無預警地身困大雷雨中。

祝你玩得盡興，打得安全！

(W)ord List

think ahead 預先設想
SPF 防曬係數（Sun Protection Factor 的縮寫，係數愈高愈能阻隔陽光中造成皮膚曬傷的 UVB 射線）
adequate [`ædəkwɪt] *adj.* 足夠的；適當的

ray [re] *n.* （輻）射線；光線
essential [ɪ`sɛnʃəl] *adj.* 必要的；基本的
lightning [`laɪtnɪŋ] *n.* （不可數）閃電
get/be caught in something 受困於某事；陷於某事
thunderstorm [`θʌndəˌstɔrm] *n.* 大雷雨

5 實戰演練 Practice Exercises

I 請為下列三題選出最適本章的中文譯義。

❶ work on...

(A) 加強…… (B) 研究…… (C) 從事……

❷ go with...

(A) 與……搭配 (B) 和……一起去 (C) 選擇使用

❸ play through

(A) 過關 (B) 超前 (C) 打完

II 你會如何回答下列這兩句話？

❶ What's your handicap?

(A) I don't hear very well. What's yours?

(B) Being too short.

(C) I'm a seven. What about you?

❷ Let's ask these guys if they'd mind if we play through.

(A) Yeah. They're slow, aren't they?

(B) I doubt they'll want to play with us.

(C) Now, watch this drive.

III 你正和一位客戶在打高爾夫球。你第二次推桿沒進，表示如果你下一個推桿再不成功的話，你將高於標準桿兩桿。你想評論一下果嶺的地形弧度和你的推桿問題。請利用下列詞語寫出一則簡短的論述：

green	slope	double bogey	putt
hole	work on	short game	

＊解答請見 237 頁

第13章
溫泉／水療
Hot Springs/The Spa

Asian countries situated around the area known as the "Ring of Fire" are often blessed with an abundance of natural hot springs. Hot spring resorts are a popular draw for people looking to relax and enjoy the therapeutic effects of the mineral-rich water. Taking a guest to soak in a hot spring can do wonders for the mind and body, soothing tired muscles and easing the pressures of a hectic work schedule.

位於被稱爲「火環」地區周圍的亞洲國家通常蘊含著豐富的天然溫泉。溫泉勝地對想要放鬆並享受豐富礦物質水療效果的人來說是相當受歡迎、極具吸引力的地方。帶客人去泡溫泉能爲身心帶來良效、安撫疲勞的肌肉，並減輕緊湊的工作行程所帶來的壓力。

1 Biz 必通句型 Need-to-Know Phrases

 CD II-17

1.1 溫泉 Hot Springs

❶ There is nothing more relaxing than....
沒有什麼比……更能讓人放鬆了。
例 There is nothing more relaxing than a day at the spa.
沒有什麼比一天的水療更能讓人放鬆了。

如果這是客人第一次泡溫泉，你應該先帶他們熟悉一下環境。

❷ You can lock your... in the locker—it/they should be safe.
您可以把……鎖在置物櫃裡——東西應該很安全。
例 You can lock your wallet in the locker—it should be safe.
您可以把皮夾鎖在置物櫃裡——東西應該很安全。

❸ I don't know if you should leave your... in the locker —it/they might not be safe.
我不確定您是否該把……留在置物櫃——可能不太安全。
例 I don't know if you should leave your digital camera in the locker—it might not be safe.
我不確定您是否該把數位相機留在置物櫃——可能不太安全。

❹ (Somebody) can get changed (location).
（某人）可以在（地方）換衣服。
例 We can get changed in the locker room.
我們可以在更衣室換衣服。

Word List

spring [sprɪŋ] *n.* 泉
spa [spɑ] *n.* 提供礦泉水療、浴療的場所（現 spa 提供的服務非常多元，可能包括美容、按摩、身體護理等）
lock [lɑk] *v.* 鎖；上鎖

locker [`lɑkɚ] *n.* 置物櫃
get changed 換衣服（get 加形容詞或過去分詞，表示狀態的變化）
locker room [`lɑkɚ ˌrum] *n.* 有置物櫃的更衣室、衣物間

❺ (Items) are all <u>provided</u> by (the spa).
（物品）全是（水療館）提供的。
例 <u>Robes</u> and <u>slippers</u> are all provided by the spa.
浴袍和室內拖鞋全是水療館提供的。

大家都知道溫泉有益身心，但不是每個人都知道箇中原因。

❻ Bathing in spring water is said to <u>promote</u>....
泡湯據說有助……。
例 Bathing in spring water is said to promote the <u>healing</u> of respiratory diseases.
泡湯據說有助呼吸疾病的治癒。

❼ A <u>soak</u> in the spring water <u>is supposed</u> to be good for....
浸泡溫泉應該對……有益。
例 A soak in the spring water is supposed to be good for the skin.
浸泡溫泉應該對皮膚有益。

❽ The spring water is believed by some to <u>possess</u>... <u>properties</u>.
有些人相信這泉水具有……功能。
例 The spring water is believed by some to possess <u>medicinal</u> properties.
有些人相信這泉水具有療效。

Word List

provide [prə`vaɪd] *v.* 提供；供應
robe [rob] *n.* 浴袍 (=bathrobe [`bæθ͵rob])
slipper [`slɪpɚ] *n.* 室內拖鞋
promote [prə`mot] *v.* 促進；推廣
healing [`hilɪŋ] *n.* 治療；康復
respiratory diseases [rɪ`spaɪrə͵torɪ dɪ`zizɪz] *n.* 呼吸疾病

soak [sok] *n./v.* 浸泡
be supposed to V. 應該……
possess [pə`zɛs] *v.* 擁有；具有
properties [`prɑpɚtɪz] *n.* （通常複數）特性；屬性；性能
medicinal [mə`dɪsn̩l] *a.* 藥物的；有治療效果的

1.2 水療服務 Spa Services

❶ I'm <u>due</u> for a (type of service).
我該（服務類型）了。
例 I'm due for a <u>manicure</u>.
我該做手指甲護理了。

❷ I'm <u>past</u> due for a (type of service).
我逾期沒（服務類型）了。
例 I'm past due for a <u>pedicure</u>.
我逾期沒做腳指甲護理。

❸ I want to <u>treat</u> you to (type of service).
我想請您去（服務類型）。
例 I want to treat you to a foot <u>massage</u>.
我想請您去做足部按摩。

❹ A massage by (a trained <u>masseur</u>/<u>masseuse</u>) costs... for (length of time).
一次（時間長度）由（一位受過訓練的按摩師／女按摩師）做的按摩要花……。
例 A massage by a trained masseuse costs NTD 1600 for an hour.
一次一個小時由受過訓練的女按摩師所做的按摩要花新台幣1600元。

Word List

due [dju] *adj.* 應做……的；到期的
manicure [ˋmænɪͺkjʊr] *n.* 手指甲護理（可包含單純的修剪指甲至保養手部皮膚、按摩及指甲護理等）
past [pæst] *prep.* 超過；經過
pedicure [ˋpɛdɪͺkjʊr] *n.* 腳指甲護理（包含範圍同 manicure，但進行的部位在腳）

treat [trit] *v.* 請客；招待；對待
massage [məˋsɑʒ] *n.* 按摩；「馬殺雞」
masseur [məˋsʊr] *n.* （法文）專業男按摩師
masseuse [məˋsuz] *n.* （法文）專業女按摩師

可以和客人分享一下你自己曾經做過的水療服務。

❺ Some people <u>swear by</u> (type of service) as a way to....
有些人深信（服務類型）是一個……的方法。
> 例 Some people swear by <u>facial mud masks</u> as a way to <u>combat</u> the signs of <u>aging</u>.
> 有些人深信泥面膜是一帖對抗老化痕跡的良方。

❻ I always feel (adj.) after a....
一次……之後，我總覺得（形容詞）。
> 例 I always feel <u>clear-headed</u> after a <u>sauna</u>.
> 一次三溫暖之後，我總覺得頭腦清楚。

❼ A (type of service) never <u>fails to</u>....
一次（服務類型）總是能……。
> 例 A <u>jet</u> shower never fails to wake me up.
> 一次噴柱水療總是能讓我清醒。

❽ For..., <u>you can't beat</u>....
要……，什麼都比不上……。
> 例 For easing <u>sore</u> muscles, you can't beat an oil massage.
> 要減輕肌肉痠痛的話，什麼都比不上油壓按摩。

❾ I've <u>booked</u> us <u>in</u> for....
我已經幫我們兩個預約好……。
> 例 I've booked us in for manicures.
> 我已經幫我們兩個預約好手指甲護理。

Ｗord List

swear by sth. 深信某事物（有效）
facial mud mask [ˈfeʃəl ˈmʌd ˌmask] n. 泥巴面膜
combat [ˈkɑmbæt] v. 戰鬥；搏鬥
ag(e)ing [ˈedʒɪŋ] n. 老化
clear-headed [ˈklɪr ˈhɛdɪd] adj. 頭腦清楚的
sauna [ˈsaʊnə] n. 三溫暖（台灣的設備一般有蒸氣室 steam room、烤箱房 dry-heat room 和不同溫度的按摩浴池 jacuzzi [dʒəˈkuzi] n.）

fail to V. 沒有能夠……
jet [dʒɛt] n. 噴射水柱；噴射氣流
you can't beat sth. 什麼都比不上……
（=there's nothing better than...）
sore [sor] adj. 痠痛的；疼痛的
book sb. in 幫某人預約（旅館、服務等）

2 實戰會話 Show Time

2.1 Hot Springs

CD II-18

John and Terry have decided to <u>head</u> up into the hills outside the city to spend a few relaxing hours at a hot spring <u>resort</u>. Terry has never been to a natural hot spring before.

John: I'll tell you, there is nothing more relaxing than a long soak in a hot spring.

Terry: I'm looking forward to it. I'm glad I <u>brought</u> my swimsuit <u>along</u>.

John: Here's a towel and some <u>flip-flops</u>—they're all provided by the resort. This resort isn't famous, but it's one of my favorites. The springs are outdoors, so you can look at the mountains while you soak.

Terry: Sounds great. So where do I <u>put on</u> my swimsuit?

John: You can get changed in the <u>change room</u> through this door. I'll meet you outside in the springs.

Terry: What's the key for?

John: Oh, that's for your locker. You can lock your <u>belongings</u> in the locker—they should be safe.

Terry: But then where do I put the key?

John: Just hang it over your neck, so you don't lose it.

Terry: OK. See you in a couple of minutes.

溫泉

約翰和泰瑞決定前往市郊的山上，到一間溫泉會館放鬆幾個小時。泰瑞以前從來沒洗過天然溫泉。

約翰：我告訴你，沒有什麼比久泡溫泉更能讓人放鬆的了。

泰瑞：我很期待。真高興我帶了泳褲來。

約翰：這裡有條毛巾和夾腳拖鞋──這些都是會館提供的。這間會館不是很有名，但它是我的最愛之一。泉水是露天的，所以你在泡的時候可以看山。

泰瑞：聽起來很棒。那我要在哪裡換泳褲？

約翰：你可以在這扇門進去的更衣室換，我會在外面的溫泉裡等你。

泰瑞：這把鑰匙是做什麼的？

約翰：喔，那是用來鎖你的置物櫃的。你可以把你的個人物品鎖在置物櫃裡──東西應該會很安全。

泰瑞：這樣我要把鑰匙放哪？

約翰：把它戴在脖子上，這樣才不會弄丟。

泰瑞：好，幾分鐘後見。

Word List

head [hɛd] *v.* 朝……前進

resort [rɪˋzɔrt] *n.* 度假之處；觀光勝地（人們尋求放鬆、遊憩前往的度假地，為自然風景名勝區或大型人工開發遊樂園地，常被借指度假飯店或大型服務會館）

bring someone/sth. along 帶著某人/某物在身邊

flip-flops [ˋflɪp͵flɑps] *n.*（通常複數）人字型的夾腳塑膠拖鞋 (= thongs [θɔŋz] *n.*)

put on [ˋpʊt͵ɑn] *phr. v.* 穿上；戴上

change room [ˋtʃɛndʒ͵rum] *n.* 更衣室

belongings [bəˋlɔŋɪŋz] *n.*（複數形）個人所有物

2.2 Spa Services

Terry and John have had enough time to soak in the hot spring. But their day of R&R is not over yet.

Terry: I feel so good after that. Honestly, I feel like a new man.

John: For recharging the batteries, you can't beat a day at the spa. A hot spring bath never fails to make me feel like I can take on the world.

Terry: I don't want to go back to the office....

John: We're not going yet. I want to treat you to a massage. I've booked us both in for half-hour massages. You're gonna love it. There are so many different kinds. They've got Swedish, Acupressure, Shiatsu, Deep Tissue, Tui Na..., whatever you want.

Terry: Awesome! I always feel wonderful after a massage.

John: What kind do you have in mind?

Terry: I don't know yet. I'll let you know when we get there.

John: Well, let's go!

水療服務

泰瑞和約翰已經泡夠溫泉，但他們的「休憩日」還沒有結束。

泰瑞：泡完之後我覺得真舒服。老實說，我覺得煥然一新。

約翰：要充電的話，什麼都比不上一天的水療。洗一次溫泉總是能讓我覺得自己能夠應付全世界。

泰瑞：我不想回辦公室了……。

約翰：我們還沒要回去，我想請您去按摩，我已經幫我們兩個預約好半個小時的按摩，您一定會喜歡。有很多種不同的類型，他們有瑞典式、穴道按摩、日式指壓、深層組織、推拿……，任君挑選。

泰瑞：太棒了！每次按摩後，我都覺得全身舒暢。

約翰：您想做哪一種呢？

泰瑞：我現在還不知道。等我們到那裡，我再跟你說。

約翰：好，那我們走吧。

Ｗord List

R&R（Relax & Recreation 的縮寫）放鬆休息不工作的一段（度假）時間
recharge [ri`tʃɑrdʒ] v. 再充電
take on [ˌtek `ɑn] phr. v. 與……對抗；接受（困難的）工作；承擔責任
Swedish [`swidɪʃ] adj. 瑞典的；瑞典語的；瑞典人的（Swedish Massage 瑞典式按摩為深層全身按摩，有助血液循環及紓解緊繃的肌肉）
acupressure [`ækjuˌprɛʃɚ] n. 中式穴道按摩（即指壓，音譯為 Zhi Ya，針對人體穴道施壓）
shiatsu [ʃi`ɑtsu] n. 日式指壓（以手指和掌心施壓身體的特定部位以達到保健養生的效果）
deep tissue [`dip `tɪʃu] n. 深層組織（Deep Tissue Massage 深層組織按摩為針對關節、特定肌肉、肌肉群由淺至軟組織深層的按摩）
Tui Na 推拿（亦針對穴道，但強調推、摩、搓、滾按等手法）
awesome [`ɔsəm] adj.（口語）太棒了！

3 Biz 加分句型 Nice-to-Know Phrases

CD II-19

3.1 選擇 Making Choices

❶ If you...,... spa will best suit your needs.
如果你……，……水療館將最符合您的需求。

例 If you don't have much time to spare, a <u>day spa</u> will best suit your needs.
如果你沒有很多時間可以用的話，一間都會型水療館將最符合您的需求。

❷ If you're not comfortable with..., they have....
如果你不習慣……，他們有……。

例 If you're not comfortable with soaking with others, they have <u>hot tubs</u> for <u>individuals</u>.
如果你不習慣和他人共浴，他們有個人專用池。

❸ This spa resort provides <u>a</u> wide <u>range of</u> services....
這家溫泉會館提供很多種服務，……。

例 This spa resort provides a wide range of services, including <u>acupuncture</u> and <u>scalp</u> massage.
這家溫泉會館提供很多種服務，包括針灸和頭皮按摩。

❹ ... is/are common in most... spas. The price for....
……在大部分的……水療館很常見。價格……。

例 Body <u>bleaching</u> and hair <u>removal</u> are common in most skin spas. The price for a <u>luxury</u> <u>package</u> varies from NTD 1800 to NTD 5400.
身體漂白和除毛在大部分的護膚水療館很常見。一套頂級療程的價格從新台幣 1800 元到新台幣 5400 元不等。

Word List

day spa[`de ˌspɑ] *n.* 都會型水療館（針對緊張的都市節奏提供顧客數小時可完成的療程，因爲一天內可完成，所以稱爲 "day spa"）

hot tub [`hɑt ˌtʌb] *n.* （熱水）按摩浴缸；按摩浴池 (= jacuzzi)

individual [ˌɪndə`vɪdʒuəl] *n.* 個人；*adj.* 個人的

a range of... 一系列的……；一批……
acupuncture [`ækjuˌpʌŋktʃɚ] *n.* 針灸
scalp [skælp] *n.* 頭皮
bleach [blitʃ] *v.* 漂白；使脫色
removal [rɪ`muvl] *n.* 除去；移除
luxury [`lʌkʃərɪ] *n.* 奢華；奢侈
package [`pækɪdʒ] *n.* 一組事物；一套行程

3.2 付帳 Paying the Bill

有時候客人會搶著付帳，下面幾句話是比較婉轉的拒絕方式，同時幫你把帳單搶回來。

❶ **Please—it's my treat.**
拜託——我請客。

❷ **It's on me.**
算我的。

❸ **You're my guest—let me look after it.**
您是我的客人——我來就好。

❹ **I'm treating—I insist.**
我請客——我堅持。

❺ **I'll get it.**
我來買單。

❻ **My boss will kill me if I let you pay.**
如果我讓您付的話，我的老闆會殺了我。

❼ **You know, my boss will <u>be mad at</u> me if I let you treat me.**
你知道的，我老闆會生我的氣，如果我讓您請的話。

ord List

be mad at sb. 對某人不高興；生某人的氣

4 Biz 加分字彙 Nice-to-Know Vocabulary

CD II-20

❶ **facial scrub** [ˈfeʃəl ˌskrʌb] *n.* 臉部去角質；臉部磨砂膏

❷ **body peeling** [ˈbɑdɪ ˌpilɪŋ] *n.* 身體去角質；身體磨砂膏

❸ **cellulite** [ˈsɛljulaɪt] *n.* 脂肪團；橘皮組織；蜂窩組織

❹ **rejuvenate** [rɪˈdʒuvənet] *v.* 使……年輕；使……恢復活力

❺ **aprés-sun treatment** [ɑˈprɛ ˈsʌn ˈtritmənt] *n.* 曬後治療

❻ **aromatherapy** [ˌærəməˈθɛrəpɪ] *n.* 芳香療法（利用精油、香料來減壓或治療）

❼ **naturopathy** [ˌnetʃəˈrɑpəθɪ] *n.* 自然療法（採取自然取向及利用自然界物質治療疾病或保健養生的方法，有別打針、吃藥的西方主流醫學，刮痧、針灸、瑜珈、藥浴等都是）

❽ **therapist** [ˈθɛrəpɪst] *n.* 治療師；特定療法技師

❾ **essential oil** [ɪˈsɛnʃəl ˈɔɪl] *n.* 精油

❿ **anti-stress** [ˌæntaɪˈstrɛs] *adj.* 抗壓的

⓫ **chronic gynecological diseases** [ˈkrɑnɪk dʒaɪnəkəˈlɑdʒɪkl̩ dɪˈzizɪz] *n.* 慢性婦科疾病

⓬ **acne** [ˈæknɪ] *n.* 痤瘡；青春痘；面皰

⓭ **dermatitis** [ˌdɝməˈtaɪtɪs] *n.* 皮膚炎

⓮ **rheumatic diseases** [ruˈmætɪk dɪˈzizɪz] *n.* 風濕病

⓯ **blood circulation** [ˈblʌd ˌsɝkjəˈleʃən] *n.* 血液循環

::::::::: 小心陷阱 :::::::::

☹ 錯誤用法

We have to wear **bath hats.**

我們必須戴浴帽。

☺ 正確用法

We have to wear **bathing caps.**

我們必須戴浴帽。

::::::::: 文化小叮嚀 :::::::::

Remember to make sure your guests remove any <u>silver jewelry</u> before bathing in hot springs—the <u>minerals</u> in the water can cause silver to <u>tarnish</u>.

When choosing a hot spring resort, keep in mind that many foreigners <u>are drawn to</u> things natural. If choosing between a resort that offers a "natural" type hot spring <u>setting</u> and another where guests sit in <u>tiled</u> "bathtubs" with spring water <u>piped</u> in, <u>opt for</u> the former—it's bound to make a more <u>favorable</u> impression.

泡溫泉之前，記得確定你的客人已脫下所有的銀飾——泉水中的礦物質會使銀飾失去光澤。

在選擇溫泉會館時，要記得很多外國人都偏愛天然的東西。如果要在一家提供「天然」溫泉環境的會館與一家讓客人坐在磁磚浴池由導管送泉水來的會館間做選擇的話，選擇前者——這樣一定會讓訪客留下更好的印象。

Ⓦord List

silver jewelry [ˌsɪlvɚ ˋʤuəlrɪ] *n.* 銀飾
mineral [ˋmɪnərəl] *n.* 礦物
tarnish [ˋtɑrnɪʃ] *v.* 使失去光澤
be drawn to... 受……的吸引
setting [ˋsɛtɪŋ] *n.* 裝飾擺設；佈景；背景

tiled [taɪld] *adj.* 舖有磁磚的
pipe [paɪp] *v.* 經由導管輸送
opt for sth. [ˋɑpt ˏfɔr] 選擇某事物
favorable [ˋfevərəbl] *adj.* 獲得讚揚的；博得好感的

181

5 實戰演練 Practice Exercises

I 請為下列三題選出最適本章的中文譯義。

❶ get changed

(A) 換零錢 (B) 換車 (C) 換衣服

❷ swear by

(A) 深信 (B) 作證 (C) 對……發誓

❸ you can't beat...

(A) 你打不贏…… (B) 什麼都比不上…… (C) 你不能打……

II 你會如何回應下面這兩句話？

❶ Where can I get changed?

(A) You could try to lose some weight, for starters.

(B) You can change in the locker room through the door on your left.

(C) You could go to Thailand. They do a lot of those operations there.

❷ I've booked us in for massages.

(A) Great, I've been feeling really tense lately.

(B) Great, I need to check my messages.

(C) What kind of books do they have?

III 你和客人正準備前往水療館，客人問你泡溫泉的好處，你想根據自己的經驗和一般說法回答。請利用下列詞語寫出一則簡答：

be good for	properties	be supposed to
bathing	never fail to	nothing more relaxing

＊解答請見 238 頁

第 **14** 章

酒吧／夜店
At the Bar/Nightclub

Going for a social drink in a bar or nightclub can give a visiting guest the chance to experience the nightlife in your city. Depending on the inclinations of your guest and the demands of your work schedule, this could mean a quick happy-hour cocktail or a late night on the town.

上酒吧或夜店交際一下喝一杯能讓訪客有機會體驗體驗你的城市的夜生活。你可以依客人的喜好以及自己工作行程的需求，來一杯優惠時段的雞尾酒速戰速決，或是度過一個流連市區的遲歸夜。

1 Biz 必通句型 Need-to-Know Phrases

CD II-21

1.1 討論酒吧 Talking About the Bar

在你提議出門前，應該先問你的客人想不想去。

---

❶ Are you up for...?

您想不想……？

例 Are you up for a drink?

您想不想喝一杯？

---

❷ ... is a great place to....

……是個……的好地方。

例 The Gaslight is a great place to have a beer and watch football on the big screen TV.

「煤氣燈」是個邊喝啤酒邊從大螢幕電視收看橄欖球的好地方。

---

❸ This place caters (more/mostly) to the... crowd.

這個地方（大多是／主要是）針對……族群服務。

例 This place caters mostly to the expat crowd.

這個地方主要是針對外僑族群服務。

每個客人都不一樣，你應該懂得觀察客人的好惡。

Word List

be up for... （口語用法）樂意……；願意……

gaslight [ˋgæsˌlaɪt] n. 煤氣燈（光）

cater to [ˋketəˌtu] phr. v. 滿足……的需求；迎合……

expat [ɛksˋpæt] n./adj. 外僑（的）(=expatriate [ɛksˋpetrɪˌet])

④ They've got (a <u>pool</u> table, bar <u>trivia</u> etc.) if you're up for a game.

如果您想玩遊戲的話，他們有（一張撞球桌、酒吧益智問答等）。

例 They've got several <u>dartboards</u> if you're up for a game.

如果您想玩遊戲的話，他們有幾個飛鏢靶。

⑤ Did you want to... or...?

您想……還是……？

例 Did you want to get a table or sit at the bar?

您想坐桌子還是坐吧台？

⑥ Let's sit (location), so we can (do something/avoid doing something).

我們坐（地方），這樣我們才能（做某事／避免做某事）

例 Let's sit by the window, so we can see what's happening on the street.

我們坐窗邊，這樣我們才能看到街景。

⑦ This place is really (adj.) tonight.

這裡今晚真（形容詞）。

例 This place is really crowded and <u>smoky</u> tonight.

今晚這裡真擠，而且煙霧瀰漫。

⑧ I'll ask (somebody) to <u>put (something) on my tab</u>.

我會請（某人）把（某物）記在我的帳上。

例 I'll ask the waitress to put another bottle of <u>Scotch</u> on my tab.

我會請女服務生把另一瓶蘇格蘭威士忌記在我的帳上。

ord List

pool [pul] *n.* 撞球；池

trivia [ˋtrɪvɪə] *n.* （有關運動、電影、電視節目等的）問答益智遊戲；瑣事

dartboard [ˋdɑrtˏbɔrd] *n.* 飛鏢靶（dart [dɑrt] *n.* 飛鏢；darts *n.* （複數形，不可數）射飛鏢遊戲）

smoky [ˋsmokɪ] *adj.* 煙霧瀰漫的；煙燻口味的

put sth. on someone's tab 把某物記在某人的帳上（tab [tæb] *n.* 帳單；費用）

Scotch [skɑtʃ] *n.* 蘇格蘭威士忌（或Scotch Whisk(e)y）

1.2 點酒 Ordering the Drinks

❶ I'll have a... (on the rocks/neat/straight, no chaser).
我要一杯（加冰塊／純的／純的、不配壓酒飲料的）……。
例 I'll have an <u>ale</u> on the rocks.
我要一杯加冰塊的麥酒。

❷ I'm going to have a... in a tall glass.
我要一杯……，用高杯裝。
例 I'm going to have a Malibu <u>Rum</u> and orange juice in a tall glass.
我要一杯馬里布蘭姆酒加柳橙汁，用高杯裝。

❸ I'd like a... with... <u>on the side</u>.
我要一杯……外加……。
例 I'd like a <u>cognac</u> with water on the side.
我要一杯干邑白蘭地外加一杯水。

如果你知道客人想喝什麼，可以幫忙點。

❹ My friend would like a <u>shot</u> of....
我朋友想來一小杯……。
例 My friend would like a shot of <u>tequila</u>.
我朋友想來一小杯龍舌蘭酒。

 ord List

on the rocks 加冰塊的
neat [nit] *adj.* （酒）純的，不加冰、水或其它酒的
straight [stret] *adj.* （酒）純的，不加任何東西的
chaser [`tʃesɚ] *n.* 喝完烈酒後喝的壓酒飲料（如啤酒、水等，用以緩和酒勁）
ale [el] *n.* 麥芽（啤）酒

rum [rʌm] *n.* 蘭姆酒（用甘蔗、糖蜜釀造而成）
on the side 作配菜；另外
cognac [`konjæk] *n.* 法國科涅克區 Cognac 生產的白蘭地
shot [ʃɑt] *n.* 一小杯；一劑
tequila [tə`kilə] *n.* 龍舌蘭酒（墨西哥 Tequila 地區出產，由龍舌蘭發酵蒸餾而成的酒）

如果你的客人對酒精飲料不熟的話，你可能需要解說一下。

❺ A (name of cocktail) has (ingredient 1), (ingredient 2), and (ingredient 3).
一杯（雞尾酒名）有（成分一）、（成分二）和（成分三）。
例 Bloody Mary has vodka, tomato juice, salt and pepper.
　　一杯血腥瑪莉裡面有伏特加、番茄汁、鹽和胡椒。

❻ Let's get another....
我們再來一……吧。
例 Let's get another pitcher of beer.
　　我們再來一壺啤酒吧。

假如你們是在慶祝，一定會舉杯敬酒。

❼ A toast—to (something/somebody).
乾杯——祝（某事／某人）。
例 A toast—to yet another successful marketing campaign!
　　乾杯——祝再一次成功的行銷活動！

❽ Should we (do something) for last call?
最後一次點酒我們要不要（做某事）？
例 Should we order another round for last call?
　　最後一次點酒我們要不要再來一輪？

ord List

Bloody Mary [`blʌdɪ `mɛrɪ] n.（雞尾酒名）
血腥瑪麗
vodka [`vɑdkə] n. 伏特加酒（由小麥、黑
麥、馬鈴薯等穀類蒸餾過濾而成的無色透明
中性烈酒）
pitcher [`pɪtʃɚ] n. 冷水壺；單耳有嘴的水罐
toast [tost] n./v. 舉杯敬酒
yet [jɛt] adv. 再；更；加之

campaign [kæm`pen] n. 宣傳活動；競選活動
last call[`læst `kɔl] n. 酒館打烊前告知客人做
最後一次點酒的提醒（可能以敲鐘、閃燈等
不同方式）
round [raʊnd] n. 一輪；一回合

2 實戰會話 Show Time

2.1 Going to the Bar

John and Terry have had a long, <u>grueling</u> day, and they've decided to go to a bar, The <u>Prancing Pony</u>, located just a couple of <u>blocks</u> from the office. The plan is to have a couple of drinks while they talk about their day.

John: The Prancing Pony is a great place to catch <u>happy hour</u> and admire some of the local <u>beauties</u>.

Terry: As long as they're not <u>blaring</u> the rock n' roll so loud that we <u>can't hear ourselves think</u>....

John: It's not that kind of <u>scene</u>. This place caters more to the middle-aged business-suit crowd.

Terry: (*Laughing.*) I guess that's us..., and you're right about the women. Wow!

John: I told you! They've got bar trivia too, if you're up for a game. Did you want to get a <u>booth</u> at the back or take one of these tables?

Terry: Let's sit here so we can check out the <u>hotties</u>!

John: OK. This place is really jumping tonight. I'll try to <u>flag down</u> a waitress.

上酒吧

約翰和泰瑞度過了漫長又累人的一天，他們決定去位於離辦公室只有幾條街一家叫做「躍馬」的酒吧。他們準備喝幾杯，一方面聊聊今天發生的事。

約翰：「躍馬」是利用酒館優惠時段及欣賞本地美女的好地方。

泰瑞：只要他們不要把搖滾樂放得那麼大聲，搞得我們頭昏腦脹就好⋯⋯。

約翰：這裡不是那個樣子的。這個地方服務的對象多半是中年的西裝族族群。

泰瑞：（笑）我想就是我們了⋯⋯，而且你說的美女是真的，哇！

約翰：我說了嘛！如果您想玩遊戲的話，他們也有酒吧益智問答。您想要坐後面的雅座還是坐這裡的其中一張桌子？

泰瑞：我們坐這裡，這樣我們才能好好欣賞辣妹！

約翰：好。這裡今晚真熱鬧。我來想辦法叫一位女服務生。

Ⓦord List

grueling [ˋgruəlɪŋ] *adj.* 非常累人的；嚴苛的
prance [præns] *v.* （馬）騰躍；（人）趾高氣昂地走
pony [ˋponɪ] *n.* 小馬；矮種馬
block [blɑk] *n.* 街區；塊狀物
happy hour [ˋhæpɪ ͵aʊr] *n.* 酒館吸引客人進場的優惠時段（飲料減價或免費供應小餐點）
beauty [ˋbjutɪ] *n.* 美女；美；（非正式）極好的事物
blare [blɛr] *v.* 轟隆響
can't hear oneself think 指一個地方太吵而受到干擾導致無法專注、做事等
scene [sin] *n.* 情況；場景
booth [buθ] *n.* 餐廳雅座；投票或禱告等四周隔有屏障的小隔間；電話亭；攤棚
hottie [ˋhɑtɪ] *n.* 辣妹；猛男
flag down [͵flæg ˋdaʊn] *phr. v.* 揮手使（計程車等）停下

189

2.2 Ordering Drinks

Terry and John have stayed longer than they planned, but they're enjoying themselves. The waitress has come to the table and it's time for another round.

Waitress: Can I get you gentlemen some more drinks?

John: Let's get another round. What do you say?

Terry: Sure. But I'm going to have something different this time.

Waitress: What will it be?

Terry: Can you recommend something that's not so strong? Another glass of <u>Hennessy XO</u> would be too much. I'm not much of a <u>drinker</u> and I don't want to wake up with a <u>hangover</u>.

Waitress: What about <u>Virgin Mary</u>? A <u>nonalcoholic</u> cocktail that has tomato juice, pepper, and lemon juice. It's a Bloody Mary made without vodka.

Terry: Sounds good, that's it.

Waitress: And you, <u>cutie</u>?

John: I'll have a <u>Smirnoff</u> on the rocks.

點酒

泰瑞和約翰待得比他們預定的晚，但他們玩得很開心。女服務生來到桌邊，該是下一輪的時候了。

女服務生：我可以幫兩位男士再拿點酒來嗎？

約翰：　　我們再喝一輪，您覺得怎樣？

泰瑞：　　好啊，但這次我想來點不同的。

女服務生：那您要？

泰瑞：　　妳能推薦什麼比較不那麼猛的嗎？再一杯軒尼士XO會太多。我不太會喝酒，而且我不想早上醒來宿醉。

女服務生：聖母瑪莉怎麼樣？是一種裡面有蕃茄汁、胡椒和檸檬汁的無酒精雞尾酒。它是沒加伏特加的血腥瑪莉。

泰瑞：　　聽起來不錯，就是它了。

女服務生：你呢？帥哥？

約翰：　　我要加冰塊的思美洛。

Word List

Hennessy XO 軒尼士 XO（Hennessy 為 cognac 的製造大廠，1765 年成立）
drinker [`drɪŋkɚ] *n.* 酒徒；慣喝⋯⋯的飲者
hangover [`hæŋ,ovɚ] *n.* 宿醉
Virgin Mary [`vɝʤɪn `mɛrɪ] *n.* （雞尾酒名）聖母瑪麗
nonalcoholic [,nɑn,ælkə`hɑlɪk] *adj.* 不含酒精的
cutie [`kjutɪ] *n.* 帥哥；美眉
Smirnoff 思美洛（一家 vodka 蒸餾廠，1860年代成立於莫斯科，為利用炭過濾酒精雜質的始祖）

3 Biz 加分句型 Nice-to-Know Phrases

CD II-23

3.1 當你不喝酒時 When You're Not a Drinker

---

❶ **I don't drink alcohol. I'll have a... <u>instead</u>.**
我不喝酒，我要一⋯⋯。
例 I don't drink alcohol. I'll have a <u>caffeine-free</u> <u>diet coke</u> instead.
我不喝酒，我要一杯無咖啡因的健怡可樂。

---

❷ **I'm not much of a drinker. I'll <u>stick to</u>....**
我不太會喝酒，我還是⋯⋯好了。
例 I'm not much of a drinker. I'll stick to mineral water.
我不太會喝酒，我還是喝礦泉水好了。

---

❸ **I can't drink tonight—(reason).**
我今晚不能喝酒——（原因）。
例 I can't drink tonight—I'm <u>on medication</u>.
我今晚不能喝酒——我在吃藥。

---

❹ **I think I'll <u>pass on</u>....**
我想我會略過⋯⋯。
例 I think I'll pass on the alcohol tonight.
我想今晚我就不喝酒了。

Word List

instead [ɪn`stɛd] *adv.* 作為替代
caffeine-free [`kæfɪn `fri] *adj.* 無咖啡因的
diet coke [`daɪət ˏkok] *n.* 健怡可樂

stick to [`stɪk ˏtu] *phr. v.* 忠於⋯⋯；繼續⋯⋯
on meditation [`ɑn ˏmɛdɪ`keʃən] 服藥中
pass on sth. 略過某事物

3.2 今晚就此為止 Call It a Night

❶ I don't know about you, but I'm ready to.... （暗示應該回家了）

我不知道你怎麼樣，可是我準備……。

例 I don't know about you, Geoff, but I'm ready to call it a night.

我不知道你怎麼樣，傑夫，可是今晚我準備休兵了。

❷ We've got a big day tomorrow—we should probably....
（提議應該結束了）

明天是咱們重要的日子——我們也許應該……。

例 We've got a big day tomorrow, Lester—we should probably <u>pack</u> it <u>in</u>.

明天是咱們重要的日子，萊斯特——我們也許應該到此為止。

❸ I'm <u>wasted.</u> That's... for me. （告訴客人你已經不行且暗示應該回家了）

我不行了。那對我來說……。

例 I'm wasted. That's enough for me.

我不行了。那對我來說已經夠了。

❹ You look like....

你看起來……。

例 You look like you've <u>had your fill</u> for one night.

看來您今晚已經喝夠了。

ord List

pack in sth. （非正式）結束某事（如為代名詞則置於中間）

wasted [`westɪd] *adj.* （俚語）喝醉的；嗑了很多藥的

have one's fill 某人已經吃飽或喝足

4 Biz 加分字彙 Nice-to-Know Vocabulary

CD II-24

❶ clubbing [ˈklʌbɪŋ] *n.* 去酒吧；去夜總會

❷ lounge bar [ˈlaʊndʒ ˌbɑr] *n.* 沙發酒吧

❸ bartender [ˈbɑrˌtɛndɚ] *n.* 酒吧侍者；酒保

❹ spirits [ˈspɪrɪts] *n.* （複數形）烈酒（如 whisky 或 gin 等）

❺ liquor [ˈlɪkɚ] *n.* 烈酒

❻ gin [dʒɪn] *n.* 琴酒；杜松子酒

❼ sake [ˈsɑˈke] *n.* 清酒（由日文 さけ 英譯而來）

❽ distill [dɪsˈtɪl] *v.* 蒸餾

❾ filter [ˈfɪltɚ] *v.* 過濾

❿ charcoal [ˈtʃɑrˌkol] *n.* 炭

⓫ corkscrew [ˈkɔrkˌskru] *n.* 軟木塞開瓶器

⓬ ice bucket [ˈaɪs ˌbʌkɪt] *n.* 冰桶

⓭ V.S.O.P. (= Very Superior Old Pale) 白蘭地酒的分級，最低陳

年數四年

⓮ V.S. (=Very Special) 白蘭地酒的分級，最低陳年數兩年

⓯ X.O. (=Extra Old) 白蘭地酒的分級，最低陳年數六年

（以上陳年數採法國 Bureau National Interprofessionnel du Cognac 定義）

☹ 錯誤用法

I'd like to make **toast**－to our new partnership!

我想舉杯──敬我們的新合作關係！

☺ 正確用法

I'd like to make **a toast**－to our new partnership!

我想舉杯──敬我們的新合作關係！

:::::::: 文化小叮嚀 ::::::::

Alcohol affects individuals differently—remember to keep an eye on your guests to make sure they're comfortable. Never try to <u>pressure</u> someone to continue drinking <u>against</u> his or her wishes. And of course, remember to make sure everyone takes a taxi if they've been drinking.

Remember: it's bad form to <u>raise</u> your glass in a toast and then put your glass down again without drinking.

酒精對每個人的影響都不一樣──要記得注意你的客人，確定他們都還覺得舒服。千萬不要違反別人的意願強迫他們一直喝。而且當然，要記得確定每個人都是搭計程車，如果他們喝了酒的話。

謹記：乾杯時舉起你的杯子沒喝再放下是不禮貌的。

Word **L**ist

pressure [`prɛʃɚ] *v.* 對……施壓；*n.* 壓力
against [ə`gɛnst] *prep.* 反對；逆
raise [rez] *v.* 舉起；增加

5 實戰演練 Practice Exercises

Ⅰ 請為下列三題選出最適本章的中文譯義。

1 be up for...

(A) 能夠…… (B) 付的起…… (C) 樂意……

2 put... on my tab

(A) 把……寫在我的牌子上 (B) 把……掛上我的牌子 (C) 把……記在我的帳上

3 flag down

(A) 投降 (B) 降旗 (C) 揮手叫住

Ⅱ 你會如何回應下面這兩句話？

1 Cheers!

(A) Put it on my tab!

(B) Cheers!

(C) Wait! Let me put on my makeup.

2 Let's pack it in.

(A) Are you sure? I think it's gonna go over the weight limit.

(B) OK. We've got a busy day tomorrow.

(C) No, thanks. I already have some.

Ⅲ 酒吧裡時間漸晚，你們的服務生來到你們的桌前，問你們是否要再來一些酒並告訴你們這是最後能點酒的機會了。你們已經討論好，決定走之前再喝一杯。請利用下面的詞語寫出一篇簡答：

get another	round	last call
be going to have	on the rocks	on my tab

＊解答請見 239 頁

第 **15** 章

博物館
Museums

If you want to introduce a foreign guest to your country's culture, a museum can be a great place. Your knowing what to say as a tour guide can make the experience that much more informative and meaningful for your guest.

如果你想向外國訪客介紹你國家的文化，博物館會是非常適合的地方。如果你知道身為導遊該介紹些什麼的話，能使你的客人經由參觀獲得更多資訊，而且會讓他們覺得更有意義。

1 Biz 必通句型 Need-to-Know Phrases

CD II-25

1.1 收藏品與工藝品（第一部分）
The <u>Collection</u> and <u>Artifacts</u> (Part I)

❶ The (name of museum) <u>houses</u> a <u>magnificent</u> collection of (art/<u>objects</u> etc.) from....

（博物館名）收藏了一系列來自……的絕佳（藝術品／物品等）。

例 The National Palace Museum houses a magnificent collection of artifacts from throughout China.

國立故宮博物院收藏了一批來自中國各地的絕佳工藝品。

❷ This <u>piece</u> is a... from the... <u>Dynasty</u>.

這是一件……朝的……。

例 This piece is a <u>perfume</u> bottle from the Song Dynasty.

這是一件宋朝的香壺。

❸ This... is <u>priceless</u>.

這件……是無價之寶。

例 This Ming Dynasty <u>vase</u> is priceless.

這個明代花瓶是無價之寶。

Ⓦord List

collection [kə`lɛkʃən] *n.* 收藏（品）
artifact [`ɑrtɪ͵fækt] *n.* 手工藝品（尤指具歷史文化價值者）
house [haʊs] *v.* 儲藏；收藏
magnificent [mæg`nɪfəsənt] *adj.* 絕佳的；華麗精美的
object [`ɑbdʒɪkt] *n.* 物品；物體

piece [pis] *n.* 藝術作品；一件
dynasty [`daɪnəstɪ] *n.* 朝代；王朝
perfume [`pɝfjum] *n.* 香水；香料
priceless [`praɪslɪs] *adj.* 無價的
vase [ves] *n.* 花瓶

❹ This... is a <u>splendid</u> example of....
這件……是……的極佳代表。
例 This <u>scroll</u> is a splendid example of Chinese <u>calligraphy</u>.
這卷字畫是中國書法的極佳代表。

❺ This... was <u>excavated</u> in (year) in (place).
這……是（年）在（地方）挖掘出土的。
例 This <u>bowl</u> was excavated in 1928 in Guandong Province.
這個碗是 1928 年在廣東省挖掘出土的。

❻ This... <u>is made of/made from</u>....
這……是由……製成的。
例 This <u>priest</u>'s hand drum is made from a human <u>skull</u>.
這件祭司的手鼓是由人頭骨所製成的。

❼ This... would have been used by (person) to....
這……可能曾被（人）用來……。
例 This box would have been used by a <u>female</u> member of the <u>aristocracy</u> to hold her <u>toiletries</u>.
這個盒子可能曾被一位女性貴族成員用來裝她的梳妝用品。

❽ This... (would have) <u>served</u> a (ceremonial/<u>practical</u> /<u>decorative</u>) function.
這個……（可能曾）有一種（儀式上的／實用性的／裝飾性的）功用。
例 This <u>scepter</u> would have served a ceremonial function.
這種權杖可能曾具有一種儀式上的功用。

Ⓦord List

splendid [`splɛndɪd] *adj.* 極佳的；壯麗的
scroll [skrol] *n.* 卷軸
calligraphy [kə`lɪgrəfɪ] *n.* 書法
excavate [`ɛkskə‚vet] *v.* 挖掘
bowl [bol] *n.* 碗
be made of... 由……製成的（由成品看得出原料，如用紙做成的紙船）
be made from... 由……製成的（由成品看不出原料，如塑膠塑料由原油提煉而來）
priest [prist] *n.* 祭司；教士；僧侶

skull [skʌl] *n.* 頭骨
female [`fimel] adj./n. 女性（的）；雌性（的）
aristocracy [‚ærəs`tɑkrəsɪ] *n.* 貴族
toiletries [`tɔɪlɪtrɪz] *n.*（複數形）梳妝用品；化妝用品；盥洗用具
serve [sɝv] *v.* 適用（目的、功能等）
practical [`præktɪkl] *adj.* 實用的；實際的
decorative [`dɛkərətɪv] *adj.* 裝飾性的
scepter [`sɛptɚ] *n.* 權杖

1.2 收藏品與工藝品（第二部分）
The Collection and Artifacts (Part II)

❶ This... is a religious <u>relic</u>.

這個……是宗教遺物。

例 This <u>tortoise</u> <u>shell</u> <u>medallion</u> is a religious relic.

這個龜甲圓盤是宗教遺物。

如果你能對你們正在看的物品作更深入的解說，你的客人一定會覺得印象深刻。

❷ The <u>markings</u> <u>indicate</u> that....

這些紋路記號顯示……。

例 The markings indicate that this cup belonged to the <u>emperor</u> himself.

這些紋路記號顯示這只杯子屬於皇帝本人所有。

❸ The... is/are <u>purely</u> decorative.

這……純粹為裝飾用。

例 The mother-of-pearl <u>inlay</u> on the <u>lid</u> is purely decorative.

這蓋子上鑲的珍珠母純粹為裝飾用。

Ⓦord List

relic [`rɛlɪk] *n.* 歷史遺物；遺風

tortoise [`tɔrtəs] *n.* （陸）龜

shell [ʃɛl] *n.* 殼；甲

medallion [mɪ`dæljən] *n.* 橢圓形或圓形的裝飾設計物；大獎章

markings [`mɑrkɪŋz] *n.* （通常複數）紋路；標誌；記號

indicate [`ɪndə,ket] *v.* 表示；指出

emperor [`ɛmpərə] *n.* 皇帝；帝王

purely [`pjʊrlɪ] *adv.* 純粹地；全然

inlay [`ɪn,le] *n.* 鑲嵌物

lid [lɪd] *n.* 蓋子

❹ This... <u>dates from</u> the... century <u>A.D./B.C.</u>.
這⋯⋯源於（西元／西元前）⋯⋯世紀。
例 This <u>brooch</u> dates from the sixteenth century A.D..
這個胸針是源於 16 世紀。

❺ People in the (century/dynasty) used to ....
（世紀／朝代）的人通常⋯⋯。
例 People in the Yuan Dynasty used to wear clothing like this for special occasions.
元朝的人通常穿這樣的衣服出席特殊的場合。

❻ The... Dynasty <u>was</u> a time of.../a time <u>characterized by</u>....
⋯⋯代是一個⋯⋯的時代／一個以⋯⋯為特徵的時代。
例 The Ming Dynasty was a time of <u>relative</u> peace and <u>prosperity</u>.
明朝是一個相對安定和富庶的時代。

❼ The (Dynasty Emperor) ruled from (year) to (year).
（朝代皇帝）從（年）統治到（年）。
例 <u>Empress</u> Wu Zetien, the only female emperor, <u>ruled</u> from 690 A.D. to 705 A.D., under the name Emperor Shengshen.
女皇武則天，唯一的女皇帝，從西元 690 年統治到西元 705 年，稱號「聖神皇帝」。

❽ This... is typical of... from (a certain <u>period</u>).
這件⋯⋯是（某一時期）典型的⋯⋯。
例 This wine <u>jar</u> is typical of <u>pottery</u> from that period.
這個酒甕是那時期典型的陶器。

Ⓦord List

date from *phr. v.* 回溯至⋯⋯；源自⋯⋯
A.D. 西元⋯⋯年（為拉丁文 Anno Domini 的縮寫，即主的紀年；現常見使用 C.E.，為 Common Era 或 Christian Era 的縮寫）
B.C. 西元前（Before Christ）
brooch [brotʃ] *n.* 胸針
be characterized by... 以⋯⋯為特徵
relative [`rɛlətɪv] *adj.* 相對的；相關的

prosperity [prɑs`pɛrətɪ] *n.* 繁榮富庶；成功興旺
empress [`ɛmprɪs] *n.* 女皇；女后
rule [rul] *v.* 統治；主宰
period [`pɪrɪəd] *n.* 時代；時期
jar [dʒɑr] *n.* 甕；瓶；罐
pottery [`pɑtərɪ] *n.* 陶器；陶藝

2 實戰會話 Show Time

CD II-26

2.1 The Museum

John has brought Terry to the National Palace Museum to give him an introduction to Chinese culture. John <u>brushed up on</u> his history before Terry arrived so he could be the best tour guide he could be.

John: The National Palace Museum houses a magnificent collection of artifacts from all over Mainland China.

Terry: What a beautiful <u>sculpture</u>!

John: Oh, yes, this piece is a splendid example of <u>jade</u> carving. It was excavated in 1930 in an area near <u>present-day</u> <u>Mongolia</u>.

Terry: The <u>workmanship</u> is unbelievable.

John: This type of carving served a decorative function. Wealthy people often <u>displayed</u> them in their homes.

Terry: I wouldn't mind displaying something like that in my place.

譯 文

博物館

約翰帶泰瑞到國立故宮博物院向他介紹中華文化。泰瑞抵達之前，約翰複習了一下他的歷史，以便能成為最棒的導覽員。

約翰：國立故宮博物院收藏了一批來自全中國大陸的絕佳工藝品。

泰瑞：好美的一座雕塑！

約翰：噢，是的，這件是玉石雕刻的極佳代表。它是1930年在一個靠近現今蒙古的地區挖掘出土的。

泰瑞：這手工真是令人難以置信。

約翰：這種雕刻物具有一種裝飾的功用，有錢人常常在的家裡展示它們。

泰瑞：我倒不介意在我家展示展示像這樣的東西。

Word List

brush up on sth. 溫習某事物；複習某事物
sculpture [`skʌlptʃə] *n.* 雕塑（品）
jade [ʤed] *n.* 玉；翡翠
present-day [`prɛznt `de] *adj.* 當今的；現代的
Mongolia [mɑŋ`goljə] *n.* 蒙古
workmanship [`wɜkmən,ʃɪp] *n.* 手藝；細工；工藝（品）
display [dɪ`sple] *v./n.* 展示；陳列

2.2 The Museum (Continued)

Terry and John are continuing their tour. They are standing in front of a display <u>case</u> housing <u>ancient</u> <u>bronze</u> <u>vessels</u>.

Terry: The <u>artistry</u> of the bronze vessels is <u>remarkable</u>!

John: It is indeed. No effort was spared <u>when it came to</u> making things for the <u>Imperial</u> <u>Court</u>.

Terry: So it would have been used by the emperor?

John: Maybe, maybe not. The markings indicate that this cup belonged to someone in the Imperial Court, <u>in any case</u>.

Terry: Which dynasty is this one from?

John: This vessel dates from the Western Xia Dynasty. The Western Xia Emperor ruled from 1032 A.D. to 1227 A.D.

Terry: Thanks. (*He notices a scroll.*) How about this painting?

John: This piece is a typical painting from the Tang Dynasty. The Tang Dynasty was a time of cultural exchange and is also considered the golden age of Chinese <u>literature</u> and art. The <u>handscroll</u> you are looking at is a piece by Wang Wei, a famous poet, musician and painter.

Terry: I think I've heard of him. Isn't he called "the Poet <u>Immortal</u>?"

John: That's Li Bai, but pretty close. Wang Wei is called "the Poet <u>Buddha</u>."

博物館（續）

泰瑞和約翰繼續他們的參觀行程。他們正站在一個收藏古銅器的展示櫃前面。

泰瑞：這些銅製器皿的作工真是非凡！

約翰：的確是。論及幫宮廷製造器皿，肯定是不遺餘力的。

泰瑞：所以它可能曾被皇帝用過？

約翰：可能是，可能不是。無論如何，這些紋路記號顯示這只杯子屬於宮廷中某位人士所有。

泰瑞：這個是來自哪個朝代？

約翰：這器皿是西夏的文物。西夏皇帝從西元 1032 年統治到西元 1227 年。

泰瑞：謝謝。（*他注意到一卷字畫*）那這幅畫呢？

約翰：這是一幅典型的唐朝書畫。唐朝是一個文化交流的時代，也被認為是中國文學和藝術的黃金時期。您現在看的這幅卷軸是王維的作品，他是一位有名的詩人、音樂家及畫家。

泰瑞：我想我聽說過他。他不是被稱作「詩仙」嗎？

約翰：那是李白，但很接近。王維被稱為「詩佛」。

Word List

case [kes] *n.* 盒子；箱子
ancient [`enʃənt] *adj.* 古代的；古老的
bronze [brɑnz] *n.* 青銅（製品）
vessel [`vɛsl] *n.* 器皿（杯、碗、壺、瓶等）
artistry [`ɑrtɪstrɪ] *n.* 藝術才華；藝術性
remarkable [rɪ`mɑrkəbl] *adj.* 令人注目的；了不起的
when it comes to... 談到……；論及……

imperial [ɪm`pɪrɪəl] *adj.* 帝國的；帝王的
court [`kort] *n.* 朝廷；宮廷
in any case 無論如何
literature [`lɪtərətʃɚ] *n.* 文學；文學作品
handscroll [`hænd͵skrol] *n.* 手卷；卷軸
immortal [ɪ`mɔrtl] *n.* 不朽的人物；*adj.* 不朽的
Buddha [`budə] *n.* 佛陀；佛

3 Biz 加分句型 Nice-to-Know Phrases

CD II-27

3.1 中國歷史 Chinese History

❶ ... history <u>dates back</u>... years.
……歷史始於……年。
例 Chinese history dates back over 5000 years.
中國歷史始於五千多年前。

❷ It was the Chinese that <u>invented</u>....
……是中國人發明的。
例 It was the Chinese that invented paper and <u>gunpowder</u>.
紙和火藥是中國人發明的。

❸ ... history is <u>broken up</u> into....
……歷史分裂為……。
例 After the Tang Dynasty, Chinese history is broken up into Five Dynasties and Ten <u>Kingdoms</u>. It was a period of political <u>upheaval</u> after the Tang Dynasty.
唐朝後，中國歷史分裂為五代十國。唐朝以後是個政治動亂的時期。

❹ Most <u>historians</u> believe/consider....
大部分的歷史學家相信／認為……。
例 Most historians consider Qin Shi Huang to be China's greatest emperor, despite his <u>brutality</u> and <u>tyranny</u>.
大部分的歷史學家認為秦始皇是中國最偉大的帝王，儘管他暴虐專橫。

Word List

date back (to) *phr.v.* 始自……；回溯至……
invent [ɪnˋvɛnt] *v.* 發明；創造
gunpowder [ˋgʌn͵paʊdɚ] *n.* 火藥
break up *phr.v.* ……分裂
kingdom [ˋkɪŋdəm] *n.* 王國；帝國

upheaval [ʌpˋhivl̩] *n.* 動亂；劇變
historian [hɪsˋtorɪən] *n.* 歷史學家
brutality [bruˋtælətɪ] *n.* 殘暴
tyranny [ˋtɪrənɪ] *n.* 暴政；專橫

3.2 鑑賞文物 <u>Admiring</u> and <u>Commenting</u> on Objects

❶ You can see....

您可以看到……。

例 You can see the artist's <u>painstaking</u> attention to detail in this <u>tripod</u>.

您可以看到這個鼎細部精心雕琢的匠工。

❷ The artistry of this... is....

這件……的工……。

例 The artistry of this <u>porcelain</u> <u>basin</u> is amazing.

這件瓷盆的作工非常了不起。

❸ The artists of the time were....

當時的藝術家都……。

例 The artists of the time were <u>inspired</u> by nature and by the things they saw around them.

當時的藝術家都受大自然及周遭所見事物的啓發。

❹ Can you guess...?

您能猜……?

例 Can you guess how the artist achieved that <u>effect</u>?

您能猜猜那位藝術家是如何達成那個效果的嗎?

Ⓦord List

admire [əd`maɪr] *v.* 欣賞;稱讚
comment [`kɑmɛnt] *v.* 評論;發表意見
painstaking [`penz͵tekɪŋ] *adj.* 精細周密
的;費盡心思的
tripod [`traɪpɑd] *n.* 鼎;三腳架等三腳物

porcelain [`pɔrslɪn] *n.* 瓷;瓷器
basin [`besn] *n.* 盆
inspire [ɪn`spaɪr] *v.* 激勵;啓發
effect [ɪ`fɛkt] *n.* 效果;作用

4 Biz 加分字彙 Nice-to-Know Vocabulary

 CD II-28

1 embroidery [ɪmˋbrɔɪdərɪ] *n.* 刺繡（品）

2 papercutting [ˋpepəˏkʌtɪŋ] *n.* 剪紙

3 puppetry [ˋpʌpɪtrɪ] *n.* 木偶戲；木偶製作

4 ceramic [səˋræmɪk] *adj.* 陶器的（ceramics 陶器製造；陶器工藝）

5 pottery [ˋpɑtərɪ] *n.* 陶器；陶藝

6 cloisoneé [ˏklɔɪzəˋne] *n.* 景泰藍

7 terracotta [ˏtɛrəˋkɑtə] *n.* 赤陶

8 lacquerware [ˋlækəˏwɛr] *n.* 漆器

9 cauldron [ˋkɔldrən] *n.* 大鍋

10 stool [ˋstul] *n.* 凳子

11 shield [ˋʃild] *n.* 盾

12 dagger [ˋdægə] *n.* 匕首；短劍

13 costume [ˋkɑstjum] *n.* 服裝；戲服

14 screen [ˋskrin] *n.* 屏風；隔板；紗窗；紗門

15 cabinet [ˋkæbənɪt] *n.* 櫥；櫃

:::::::: 小心陷阱 ::::::::

☹ 錯誤用法

This jade carving is **valueless**.

這件玉雕是無價之寶。

☺ 正確用法

This jade carving is **priceless**.

這件玉雕是無價之寶。

:::::::: 文化小叮嚀 ::::::::

Many foreigners do not like to be around large tour groups, which <u>tend to</u> be noisy and can make a place crowded <u>in a hurry</u>. If you notice that such groups are touring the museum at the same time you are, your foreign guests will likely appreciate your <u>efforts</u> to <u>steer</u> them <u>away from</u> tour groups towards a quieter and less crowded corner of the museum.

很多外國人都不喜歡靠近大的參觀團,這些團通常很吵而且一下子就會把一個地方搞得擁擠不堪。如果你注意到有這樣的團體和你們同一時間參觀博物館,盡力將你的外國訪客導離參觀團體到館裡一個較安靜且較不擁擠的角落,他們應該會很感激你的用心。

Word List

tend to V. 傾向於……

in a hurry 快速地;匆忙地

effort [`ɛfət] *n.* 努力

steer away from... 導離……

5 實戰演練 Practice Exercises

I 請為下列三題選出最適本章的中文譯義。

❶ brush up on...

(A) 梳洗…… (B) 複習…… (C) 刷拭……

❷ when it comes to...

(A) 開始…… (B) 接著是…… (C) 論及……

❸ break up

(A) 分手 (B) 分裂 (C) 解散

II 你會如何回應下面這兩句話？

❶ This Ming Dynasty vase is priceless.

(A) Yes, none of the pieces in the museum's collection are for sale.

(B) I believe it—it's exquisite.

(C) Well, I don't know how much it costs.

❷ You can see the artist's painstaking attention to detail in this tripod.

(A) Oh, that must have hurt.

(B) No pain, no gain.

(C) Wow, it's hard to believe such intricate work can be done on a small object like this.

III 你和客人正在觀看一個元朝（西元1271年至西元1368年）陶土文物的展示櫃，你想向你的客人解說其中一件。請利用下列詞語寫出一篇簡介：

artifact	date from	century
be made from	would have been used to	workmanship

＊解答請見 240 頁

第 **16** 章

道別
Saying Goodbye

Your have entertained, wined and dined your guest, and now it's time to see them on their way. Going over what's been accomplished over the course of their trip and talking about the tasks that lie ahead in the days to come are part of the sendoff, just as much as wishing them a fond farewell is.

在娛樂、酒宴和美食招待過你的客人後,現在是送客人踏上歸途的時候了。審視他們這趟行程中達成的事項與討論日後將進行的任務,就像衷心祝他們一路順風一樣,都是歡送會的一部份。

1 Biz 必通句型 Need-to-Know Phrases

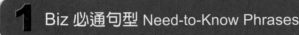

CD II-29

1.1 成果及未來計劃 Accomplishments and Future Plans

❶ I'm glad we were able to....
我很高興我們能……。
例 I'm glad we were able to get the <u>annual</u> report <u>wrapped up</u> on schedule.
很高興我們能如期順利完成年報。

❷ I'm really looking forward to....
我非常期待……。
例 I'm really looking forward to working with you on the new European <u>accounts</u>.
我非常期待能與您一起經營新的歐洲客戶。

❸ I am confident that our new (partnership/<u>arrange-ment</u>/business <u>venture</u>) is going to be (adj.) for....
我確信我們的新（合作關係／協議／投資事業）對……將會是（形容詞）。
例 I am confident that our new partnership is going to be <u>lucra-tive</u> for both companies.
我確信我們的新合作關係會為我們兩家公司都帶來很好的利潤。

❹ I think it's great we were able to <u>come to an agree-ment</u> on....
我覺得我們能達成……的協議真是太好了。
例 I think it's great we were able to come to an agreement on the <u>terms</u> of the new contract.
我覺得我們能達成新合約的條件協議真是太好了。

Word List

accomplishment [əˋkɑmplɪʃmənt] *n.* 成就
annual [ˋænjʊəl] *adj.* 一年一次的
wrap up [ˋræp ˏʌp] *phr. v.* 結束；完成（協定、會議等）
account [əˋkaʊnt] *n.* 客戶；帳戶
arrangement [əˋrendʒmənt] *n.* 安排；籌畫；協定；協議

venture [ˋvɛntʃɚ] *n.* 投機；冒險；風險投資
lucrative [ˋlukrətɪv] *adj.* 很有利潤的
come to an agreement 達成協議
terms [tɝmz] *n.* （複數形）協議、合約等的條件

❺ I'm <u>thrilled</u> that we were able to reach an understanding on....

我非常高興我們能就⋯⋯達成共識。

例 I'm thrilled that we were able to reach an understanding on the <u>billing</u> procedures.

我非常高興我們能就請款程序達成共識。

也許還有事情需要解決，你可以順便提一下。

❻ I hope we'll be able to <u>work out</u> the details about... over the next....

希望我們能在接下來的⋯⋯擬定⋯⋯的細節。

例 I hope we'll be able to work out the details about the <u>shipment</u> schedule over the next couple of weeks.

希望我們能在接下來的幾個禮拜擬定貨物裝運的日期細節。

❼ It's too bad we weren't able to..., but at least....

很遺憾我們沒能⋯⋯，但至少⋯⋯。

例 It's too bad we weren't able to come to an agreement on prices, but at least we <u>made</u> some <u>headway</u> on the <u>subcontracting</u> issue.

很遺憾我們沒能達成價格的協議，但至少我們在轉包議題上有一些進展。

❽ ... will be in touch about... (date).

⋯⋯（日期）會就⋯⋯與您聯絡。

例 Agatha Ho will be in touch about the new orders on Monday.

艾格莎・何星期一會就新訂單的事與您聯絡。

Ⓦord List

thrilled [θrɪld] *adj.* 非常開心且興奮的
bill [bɪl] *v.* 開帳單要求付款
work out [`wɝk͵aut] *phr. v.* 制訂出⋯⋯；
解決⋯⋯

shipment [`ʃɪpmənt] *n.* 貨物裝運（不僅於海運的方式）
make headway 取得進展
subcontract [sʌb`kɑntrækt] *v.* 轉包

1.2 Fond Farewells 惜別

❶ I think we can <u>safely say</u> your trip was a(n) (adj.) one.

我想我們可以穩當地說您這趟行程（形容詞）。

例 I think we can safely say your trip was a productive one.

我想我們可以穩當地說您這趟行程成效卓著。

❷ I hope you enjoyed your time here in....

我希望您在……的這段時間過得非常愉快。

例 I hope you enjoyed your time here in Taiwan.

希望您在台灣的這段時間過得非常愉快。

❸ It's a shame you won't be here for....

可惜您不會在這裡……。

例 It's a shame you won't be here for the <u>Lantern</u> Festival.

可惜您不會在這裡過元宵節。

提及你為客人再次來訪所做的計劃會讓客人感受到你的熱情，覺得你很高興他們這次來並且希望很快再見到他們。

❹ Next time, we'll have to get you out to see....

下次，我們一定要帶您去看……。

例 Next time, we'll have to get you out to see the Hanging Gardens.

下次，我們一定要帶您去看空中花園。

Ⓦord List

safely say 穩當地說；大可說

lantern [`læntɚn] *n.* 燈籠

❺ When can we expect to see you back in...?

我們能期待您什麼時候再回來……？

例 When can we expect to see you back in Guandong?

我們能期待您什麼時候再回來廣東？

❻ I suppose the next time I'll see you will be when I'm in (place) (time).

我想下次見到您應該會是（時間）我在（地方）的時候。

例 I suppose the next time I'll see you will be when I'm in Bangkok in October.

我想下次見到您應該會是十月份我在曼谷的時候。

如果有些事情是要等客人回去後才能處理的，應該稍微提醒一下。

❼ (Please) be sure to... when you get back to....

等您回到……，（請）務必……。

例 Be sure to send me that <u>invoice</u> when you get back to the <u>head office</u>.

等您回到總公司，務必把那張發票寄給我。

❽ Have a good flight—I'll talk to you when....

祝您飛行愉快——當……，我會跟您連絡。

例 Have a good flight—I'll talk to you when you <u>get to</u> Brussels.

祝您飛行愉快——當您抵達布魯塞爾後，我會跟您聯絡。

Ⓦord List

invoice [ˋɪnvɔɪs] *n.* （商業）發票；發貨單

head office [ˋhɛd ˋɔfɪs] *n.* 公司總部

get to (a place) *phr. v.* 抵達（一地）

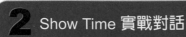

2 Show Time 實戰對話

2.1 Recapping the Trip

Terry is getting ready to go. He's standing outside his hotel with John, and they're waiting for the taxi that the concierge has just called to take Terry to the airport.

John: Well, Terry, I'm glad we were able to get the new <u>database</u> up and running.

Terry: Yeah, me too. I'm really looking forward to <u>taking advantage of</u> the new, <u>streamlined</u> <u>ordering</u> system.

John: I'm confident that our new system is going to be a big <u>time-saver</u> for everyone involved.

Terry: It's too bad we weren't able to get all the new <u>hardware</u> <u>installed</u>, but at least the staff has been trained on how to use the database.

John: Everything will be <u>in place</u> soon enough. I'll be in touch about the <u>installation</u> early next week.

Terry: Good. I'll expect your call.

譯 文

重述行程重點

泰瑞準備好要離開了。他跟約翰站在飯店外面等門房剛叫的計程車,要載泰瑞去機場。

約翰:那,泰瑞,很高興我們能讓新資料庫上線運轉。

泰瑞:是啊,我也是。我非常期待應用這套新的、簡便又有效率的訂購系統。

約翰:我確信我們的新系統對每個相關人員將是一個省時的大幫手。

泰瑞:很遺憾我們沒能把所有的新硬體都安裝好,但至少員工已經被訓練知道如何使用資料庫。

約翰:一切很快就會上軌道。我下星期初會就安裝的事與您聯絡。

泰瑞:好,我會等你的電話。

Word List

recap [ri`kæp] *v.* 重述重點
database [`detə‚bes] *n.* 資料庫
take advantage of... 利用……
streamlined [`strim‚laind] *adj.* 有效整合或簡化的;簡便又有效率的;流線型的
order [`ɔrdɚ] *v.* 訂購
time-saver *n.* 節省時間的事物(saver [`sevɚ] *n.* 節省……的事物)
hardware [`hɑrd‚wɛr] *n.*(不可數)電腦硬體
install [in`stɔl] *v.* 安裝
in place 就緒的
installation [‚instə`leʃən] *n.* 安裝;裝置;設備

1.2 A Fond Farewell

Terry's <u>cab</u> <u>pulls up</u> in the <u>circular</u> <u>drive</u> in front of the hotel. It's time to shake hands and say goodbye.

John: Here's your cab.

Terry: Right, I'm <u>off</u>! Listen, thanks for everything, John.

John: It's been my pleasure. I hope you enjoyed your time here in Hsinchu. It's a shame you won't be here for the Lantern Festival. It's a great time of year.

Terry: Yeah, I wish I could stay, but you know how it is: busy, busy, busy! It's been a great time, though—I honestly can't ever remember having so much fun on a business trip!

John: I'm glad you enjoyed yourself. So, when can we expect to see you back in Hsinchu?

Terry: Hard to say... depends on what the V.P. of Sales and Marketing decides.

John: Well, in any case, have a good flight—I'll talk to you when the installation is complete.

Terry: OK, John. And thanks again. See you next time.

John: Goodbye.

惜別

泰瑞的計程車在飯店前面的環形車道上停了下來。該是握手道別的時刻了。

約翰：您的計程車來了。

泰瑞：沒錯，我走了！聽好，約翰，一切多謝了。

約翰：這是我的榮幸。希望您在新竹的這段時間過得非常愉快。可惜您不會在這裡過元宵節，這是一年的大日子。

泰瑞：是啊，我也希望能留下來，但是你也知道是怎樣：忙、忙、忙！不過，到這兒這段時間真的很棒──老實說，我不記得出差洽商有這麼開心過！

約翰：很高興您覺得愉快。那，什麼時候我們能期待您再回來新竹？

泰瑞：很難說……要看業務行銷部副總怎麼決定。

約翰：嗯，無論如何，祝您飛行愉快──當安裝完成之後，我會跟您聯絡。

泰瑞：好，約翰。再次謝謝你，下回再見。

約翰：再見。

Word List

cab [kæb] *n.* 計程車
pull up [`pʊl ˌʌp] *phr. v.* 停下來
circular [`sɝkjələ] *adj.* 圓形的；循環的
drive [draɪv] *n.* 車道
off [ɔf] *adv.* 離開

3 Biz 加分句型 Nice-to-Know Phrases

 CD II-31

3.1 送禮 Giving a Gift

❶ Here's a little something....
這裡有一個小東西⋯⋯。
例 Here's a little something we'd like you to have as a souvenir of your stay.
這裡有個小東西我們希望您收下，作為您這次來訪的紀念品。

❷ We got you a little....
我們要給您一個小⋯⋯。
例 We got you a little <u>going-away</u> present.
我們要給您一個臨別小禮物。

❸ We'd like to present you with....
我們想贈送您⋯⋯。
例 We'd like to present you with this gift as a <u>token</u> of our esteem and <u>appreciation</u>.
我們想贈送您這個禮物，表示我們的尊敬及感謝。

❹ This is something for you....
這個東西給您⋯⋯。
例 This is something for you to help you remember your visit.
這個東西送給您，有助您記得這次的來訪。

Word List

going-away [`goɪŋ ə`we] *adj.* 離開的（go away *phr. v.*）
token [`tokən] *n.* 象徵
appreciation [ə,priʃɪ`eʃən] *n.* 感謝；賞識

3.2 道別 Saying Goodbye

相聚總有離別時，到了道別的時候了，客人踏上歸程，你的任務即將結束，用下列這四句話營造溫馨氣氛，期待下次的聚首。

❶ It's been great....
很高興……。
例 It's been really great having you here.
真的很高興您來這裡。

❷ It's been a pleasure....
很榮幸……。
例 It's been a real pleasure having you with us.
非常榮幸有您參與。

❸ I've enjoyed....
我很開心……。
例 I've really enjoyed having the chance to show you around.
我非常開心有機會帶您四處看看。

❹ I hope you've enjoyed....
我希望您滿意……。
例 I hope you've enjoyed your visit as much as we've enjoyed having you.
希望您對您這次的來訪感到滿意，就像我們很高興有您來訪一樣。

4 Biz 加分字彙 Nice-to-Know Vocabulary

CD II-32

① **prospectus** [prəˋspɛktəs] *n.*
（學校、企業等的）簡章、宣傳資料

② **pro forma invoice** [ˌpro ˋfɔrmə ˋɪnvɔɪs] *n.* 形式發票；估價單

③ **quotation** [kwoˋteʃən] *n.* 估價單；報價；引文

④ **letter of credit** [ˋlɛtɚ əv ˋkrɛdɪt] *n.* (=L/C) 信用狀

⑤ **bill of lading** [ˋbɪl əv ˋledɪŋ] *n.* (=B/L) 提貨單

⑥ **shipping order** [ˋʃɪpɪŋ ˋɔrdɚ] *n.* (=S/O) 裝貨單

⑦ **packing list** [ˋpækɪŋ ˋlɪst] *n.* 包裝明細表

⑧ **sales confirmation** [ˋselz ˌkɑnfɚˋmeʃən] *n.* 銷貨確認書

⑨ **delivery** [dɪˋlɪvərɪ] *n.* 交貨；遞送

⑩ **consignment** [kənˋsaɪnmənt] *n.* 託運；運送

⑪ **freight** [fret] *n.* 貨物，運費，運貨；*v.* 運送

⑫ **crate** [kret] *n.* (運貨用的)大木箱；板條箱

⑬ **remittance** [rɪˋmɪtn̩s] *n.* 匯款；匯款額

⑭ **sister company** [ˋsɪstɚ ˋkʌmpənɪ] *n.* 姊妹公司

⑮ **subsidiary** [səbˋsɪdɪˌɛrɪ] *n.* 子公司；*adj.* 輔助的，次要的

┌─────────────── 小心陷阱 ───────────────┐

☹ 錯誤用法

I'm looking forward to **work** with you.

我很期待與您共事。

☺ 正確用法

I'm looking forward to **working** with you.

我很期待與您共事。

└──────────────────────────────────────┘

┌─────────────── 文化小叮嚀 ───────────────┐

If you're going to give a going-away gift, remember that certain types of food (like fruits and vegetables) often cannot be imported into another country without special permission.

Another thing to keep in mind when giving a gift is that in most Western countries it is considered bad form to mention how much you paid for a gift. If, for some reason, you really want the recipient to know how much you paid, simply make a point of "accidentally" not removing the price sticker.

如果你要送臨別禮物，記得某些種類的食物（像是水果及蔬菜）如果沒有特別許可的話，通常不能帶進另一個國家。

另一件送禮時需謹記於心的事是，在大部分的西方國家，提及你花多少錢買一件禮物會被視為是失禮的表現。如果，為了某個理由，你真的希望收禮者知道你花了多少錢，那就刻意「意外地」不要撕掉價格標籤就行了。

└──────────────────────────────────────┘

ord List

recipient [rɪ`sɪpɪənt] *n.* 收領者

sticker [`stɪkɚ] *n.* 貼紙；黏貼標籤

make a point of doing sth. 刻意做某事

實戰演練 Practice Exercises

I 請為下列兩題選出最適本章的中文譯義。

❶ work out

(A) 健身 (B) 擬定 (C) 開發

❷ make headway

(A) 領先 (B) 創新 (C) 有進展

II 你會如何回應下面這兩句話？

❶ I'll be in touch about the new orders on Monday.

(A) I won't touch them before then.

(B) I'll be waiting to hear from you then.

(C) OK, I'll call you Monday.

❷ It's been a pleasure having you here.

(A) You can say that again!

(B) The pleasure is mine.

(C) I think the same.

III 幾天協商、會議之後，你要跟客人說再見了，但還有些未定事項需等客人回辦公室之後再處理，請利用下列詞語寫出一則簡短的提醒：

we can safely say　　　reach an understanding　　　be in touch

work out the details　　final draft

＊解答請見 241 頁

實戰演練
Answer Keys

Chapter  接機

I　1. (B)　2. (C)　3. (B)

II　1. (B)　2. (C)

❶ 我梳洗一下就會覺得好多了。

(A) 是的，沒有比走味更糟的事了。

(B) 那邊有間化妝室——您慢慢來。

(C) 請稍微處理一下你那股體味。

❷ 我實在累慘了！

(A) 是啊，你看起來就像有人在你臉上揍了一拳。

(B) 我下棋很少輸。

(C) 你何不回飯店小睡一下？

III 範例解答：

You: Tina, we're coming up on old City Hall. If you want, we can stop along the way and you can take some pictures.

Tina: No, thanks. I'd prefer to go directly to the office. I can take pictures later.

你　：緹娜，我們快到舊市府了。如果妳要的話，我們可以停下來讓妳拍些照片。

緹娜：不，謝了，我想直接去辦公室。我可以晚一點再拍。

stale [stel] *adj.* 不新鮮的；腐壞的；污濁的

odor [`odɚ] *n.* 氣味；香氣；臭氣

Chapter 2 飯店

I 1. (A) 2. (C) 3. (A)

II 1. (B) 2. (A)

❶ 看來您好像都準備好了。

(A) 是啊，我也覺得十分驚訝。

(B) 是啊，我需要的都有了。

(C) 是啊，我無法動彈。

❷ 上次我住這家飯店時，他們早上七點半就用吸塵器打掃我房外的走廊。

(A) 別擔心——我會關照櫃檯人員以確保這次不會再發生同樣的事。

(B) 別擔心——他們只是清潔人員。

(C) 別擔心——市區還有幾家不錯的飯店我可以推薦。

III 範例解答：

Ed: I don't speak a word of Chinese. I hope I won't have any problems.

You: Don't worry, Mr. Morris. All the staff here speaks English as well as Chinese. You can call the front desk if you need anything at all. They'll be happy to arrange for what you need.

愛德：我半句中文也不會說，希望不會有什麼問題。

你　：別擔心，莫里斯先生。這裡所有的員工都會講英語和中文。假如您有任何需要，可以打電話給櫃台，他們會十分樂意幫您安排您所需要的東西。

Chapter
3 介紹

I 1. (C) 2. (A) 3. (B)

II 1. (B) 2. (A)

❶ 我讓你們單獨聚聚敘敘舊。

　(A) 為什麼？我們的進度又落後了嗎？

　(B) 好，我待會再跟你聊。

　(C) 請不要不理我們。

❷ 東尼奧和我早就認識了。

　(A) 真的嗎？你們兩個在哪認識的？

　(B) 回去哪裡？

　(C) 真的嗎？真希望你們不要這麼早走。

III 範例解答：

You:　　Mr. May, I don't believe you've met Michael Cheng. Michael is one of our top patent engineers. We have known each other since our university days.

Curtis:　Hi Michael, I'm Curtis.

Michael: Pleased to meet you, Curtis.

You:　　Mr. May is in town for the electronics trade fair. This party will be a good chance for us to talk about the layout of our display.

你　　：梅先生，我相信您還沒見過麥可・鄭。麥可是我們數一數二的專利工程師，我們打從大學時代就認識了。

克提斯：嗨，麥可，我是克提斯。

麥可　：很高興認識你，克提斯。

你　　：梅先生是來參加電子商展的。這個派對將是我們討論展覽該如何設計的好機會。

Chapter 4 咖啡店和茶館

I 1. (B) 2. (B)

II 1. (B) 2. (C)

❶ 你的咖啡要加什麼？

(A) 我早上帶去上班。

(B) 我喝黑咖啡——不用奶精或糖。

(C) 我用杯子裝，大家不都這樣嗎？

❷ 這種咖啡來自哪裡？

(A) 這種咖啡外銷到世界各地。

(B) 從櫃台後面的那只大咖啡罐來的。

(C) 這種咖啡是從巴西進口的。

III 範例解答：

The coffee of the day is Italia D'Oro blend. It says it's a dark roast with a hearty aroma and a rich, full-bodied flavor. Care to give it a try?

本日咖啡是義大利多羅綜合咖啡。上面寫說它是深度烘焙，具有濃厚的香味和濃郁、醇重的口感。要不要試試看？

Chapter
5　正式晚宴／宴會

I　1. (A)　2. (C)　3. (C)

II　1. (C)　2. (B)

❶ 我把你的酒杯斟滿好嗎？
　(A) 我比較希望你喝你自己的。
　(B) 我想它撐不了你的重量。
　(C) 我再來一點點，謝謝。
❷ 您將坐在主桌。
　(A) 我以前從來沒吃過頭。
　(B) 我很榮幸。
　(C) 我得把頭擺在哪裡？

III 範例解答：

Tonight's banquet will be very special. We're having a seven-course meal of Sri Lankan cuisine. The appetizer is a kind of flatbread, and the main course is a chicken curry. I'm not sure what we're having for dessert.

今晚的宴會將會非常特別，我們要享用七道菜的斯里蘭卡料理。前菜是一種扁麵包，主菜是咖哩雞，我不確定甜點會上什麼。

Chapter
6 參觀工廠

I　1. (C)　2. (C)

II　1. (A)　2. (B)

❶ 對公司也一定有利。

　(A) 當然──省了這麼多。

　(B) 是的，我們花錢搞定城裡每一個人，包括警察。

　(C) 是的，我們的員工每隔週五領薪一次。

❷ 我們提供極具競爭力的薪資和福利。

　(A) 說穿了就是「適者生存」而已。

　(B) 這裡的工作環境似乎也很好。

　(C) 你們的員工似乎很喜歡互相競爭。

III 範例解答：

Quests: Where do your materials come from?

You:　We import a lot of ingredients from Europe and incorporate them into our recipes. We insist on using only the finest ingredients, and we have stringent quality controls in place to make sure our customers get the very best.

客人：　你們的原料來自何處？

你　：　我們從歐洲進口很多原料並將它們融入我們的製作方式。我們堅持只用最精緻的原料，而且我們實施嚴格的品管以確保我們的顧客獲得最好的東西。

Chapter 7 購物

I 1. (B) 2. (A) 3. (B)

II 1. (B) 2. (B)

❶ 他們缺貨。

(A) 太好了！我要三個。

(B) 好可惜！

(C) 他們應該坐下來休息一下。

❷ 我在找買特定的品牌。

(A) 我以前也玩樂團。

(B) 哪個牌子？

(C) 你一定要這麼挑嗎？

III 範例解答：

This antique market is great—you'll be able to pick up some gifts for your friends and family here. But I should tell you: you have to bargain. All the prices are negotiable, but the vendors are very shrewd business people. I wouldn't pay more than two-thirds of the asking price if I were you.

這個骨董市場很棒——您應該能在這裡挑到一些禮物給親友。但我應該告訴您：您一定要殺價。所有的價格都是可以商量的，不過這些商家都是十分精明的生意人。如果是我的話，超過要價三分之二我就不會買。

vendor [`vɛndɚ] *n.* 小販
shrewd [ʃrud] *adj.* 精明的；狡猾的

Chapter 8 上 KTV

Ⅰ 1. (B) 2. (A) 3. (C)

Ⅱ 1. (B) 2. (A)

❶ 一個晚上唱下來你覺得夠了嗎？

(A) 你說的是哪一晚？

(B) 還沒呢——我們再待一會。

(C) 我比較喜歡在白天唱歌。

❷ 喝一杯，讓自己像在家裡一樣。

(A) 謝了，別介意我照作喔。

(B) 但我還不想回家。

(C) 謝了，可是我在家不調酒的。

Ⅲ 範例解答：

Oh, I love this song—it's a classic! I'm a sucker for the oldies, especially American rock and roll from the 50s. It's practically all I listen to these days.

噢，我愛這首歌——它很經典！我是懷舊歌曲迷，尤其是 50 年代的美國搖滾樂。我最近幾乎只聽這種歌。

oldie [`oldɪ] *n.* （非正式）老歌；老影片；老人

Chapter
9 夜市

I 1. (C) 2. (C) 3. (C)

II 1. (C) 2. (A)

---

❶ 以我的口味來說這道「水牛城雞翅」有點太辣了。

(A) 別擔心，如果你持續規律運動的話就不會變胖。

(B) 這裡有調味料。

(C) 那裡有座飲水機。你下次或許還是吃牛肉好了。

❷ 我必須承認我抗拒不了油炸食物。

(A) 在夜市吃油炸食物，可以稱為是「充滿罪惡感的享受」。

(B) 勇於承認並不是軟弱的象徵。

(C) 它也讓我覺得很虛弱。

III 範例解答：

That stall is selling fried squid. It's a popular local delicacy. The squid is chopped into strips and dipped in batter before it's fried in oil. After it's fried, the vendor will add basil as a garnish.

那攤在賣炸魷魚，那是一道相當受歡迎的本地美食。魷魚在油炸之前會先被切成條狀並沾裹麵糊。炸好後，小販會放上羅勒（九層塔）作為裝飾佐料。

---

workout [`wɝk͵aʊt] *n.* 運動；健身

water fountain [`wɔtɚ ͵faʊntn̩] *n.* 飲水機 (=drinking fountain)

stick with sth. 忠於某事物（不選擇他物）

basil [`bæzɪl] *n.* 羅勒（別名：九層塔，味道強烈的芳香藥草，常用作烹飪佐料或用於芳香療法中；台灣所植的九層塔風味及種類與歐美的不同）

Chapter 10 語言

I 1. (B) 2. (C) 3. (C)

II 1. (A) 2. (B)

❶ 我在莫斯科的時候，學了一點點的「活命」俄語。

   (A) 好厲害。俄文難嗎？

   (B) 我一直很好奇想知道俄國人是如何學會求生的。

   (C) 哇！所以你已經很流利了！

❷ 你的母語是什麼？

   (A) 我媽媽說台語和國語。

   (B) 我從小在家說台語長大。

   (C) 你剛說我媽媽的舌頭怎樣？

III 範例解答：

This character is pronounced "shān" —first tone. It means "mountain." Doesn't this part look like a mountain peak? It's one of the simplest characters—only four strokes.

這個字唸作「ㄕㄢ」——一聲，「山」的意思。這部分看起來不就像是一座山峰嗎？這是最簡單的字之一——只有四劃。

Chapter
11 廟宇

I 1. (C) 2. (A) 3. (B)

II 1. (C) 2. (A)

❶ 這場繞境是在紀念媽祖誕辰。

(A) 我等不及要看那些活力四射的啦啦隊員了！

(B) 她一定是個重要又有錢的人。

(C) 我們可以停幾分鐘嗎？我想瞭解一下是怎麼樣的。

❷ 我們的衣著適合進去嗎？

(A) 適合，但你應該先脫掉帽子。

(B) 我們為什麼要穿禮服？

(C) 我喜歡你的這身行頭。

III 範例解答：

This painting commemorates the enlightenment of the Buddha. The belief that Buddha attained enlightenment, and that we all can do the same, is a central tenet of Buddhism. The tree Buddha is sitting under, with its many branches, represents the illusory nature of the material world.

這幅畫是在紀念佛陀悟道。相信佛陀成道，及一切眾生也都能如此，是佛教的主要教義。佛陀坐於其下的那棵樹，和它眾多的樹枝，代表物質世界的虛幻本質。【佛陀成道日──法寶節，為農曆 12 月 8 日】

enlightenment [ɪn`laɪtn̩mənt] *n.* 啟蒙；
（佛家語）菩提 bodhi，即「覺、智、悟」
attain [ə`ten] *v.* 達到；獲得
branch [bræntʃ] *n.* 樹枝；分支

illusory [ɪ`lusərɪ] *adj.* 幻象的；幻覺的
nature [`netʃɚ] *n.* 本質；本性
material world [mə`tɪrɪəl `wɝld] *n.* 物質世界

Chapter

12 高爾夫球場

I　1. (A)　2. (C)　3. (B)

II　1. (C)　2. (A)

❶ 你的差點是多少？

(A) 我的聽力不太好。你的呢？

(B) 太矮。

(C) 我是七。你呢？

❷ 我們來問問這些人，看他們介不介意我們超前先打。

(A) 好啊。他們打得很慢，不是嗎？

(B) 我懷疑他們會想跟我們打。

(C) 現在，注意看這記開球。

III 範例解答：

Missed again! That's going to give me a double bogey on this hole if I don't make this next putt. The green slopes more than I thought it did. I really need to work on my short game!

又沒進！如果這一桿再沒推進的話，那我這洞就是雙柏忌了。這果嶺比我想的還要陡。我真的需要再加強一下我的短桿了！

short game [ˋʃɔrt ˌgem] *n.* 短桿（指離果嶺 100 碼內的擊球，如沙坑球、切球、推桿等）

Chapter 13　溫泉／水療

I　1. (C)　2. (A)　3. (B)

II　1. (B)　2. (A)

❶ 我要在哪裡換衣服？

(A) 首先，您可以試著減重。

(B) 您可以在由您左手邊那扇門進去的更衣室裡換。

(C) 您可以去泰國，他們那裡有很多這樣的手術。

❷ 我已經幫我們兩個預約好按摩了。

(A) 太好了！我最近一直覺得很緊繃。

(B) 太好了！我需要看一下我的來件。

(C) 他們有哪些種類的書？

III 範例解答：

Hot spring water is good for the skin. The mineral properties of the water are supposed to smooth the skin. I don't know if that's true or not, but I know bathing in a hot spring never fails to make me feel wonderful. For my money, there's nothing more relaxing.

溫泉水對皮膚有益。一般認為泉水中的礦物特性可以使皮膚光滑。我不知道是真的還是假的，但我知道泡溫泉總是能讓我覺得全身舒暢。依我看，沒有什麼可以讓人更放鬆的了。

for my money 依我看（用來強調自己接著要說的話是正確的）

Chapter 14 酒吧／夜店

I 1. (C) 2. (C) 3. (C)

II 1. (B) 2. (B)

❶ 乾杯！

(A) 把它記在我的帳上！

(B) 乾杯！

(C) 等一下！讓我化一下妝。

❷ 我們到此為止吧。

(A) 你確定？我覺得會超過重量限制。

(B) 好，我們明天還有得忙呢。

(C) 不，謝了。我已經有一些了。

III 範例解答：

We'll get another round for last call. I'm going to have another beer, and my friend here will have a gin and tonic, on the rocks. Can you put it on my tab please?

最後一次點酒我們要再來一輪。我要再來一杯啤酒，我這位朋友要一杯琴湯尼，加冰塊。能不能請你把它記在我的帳上？

gin and tonic [`dʒɪn ənd `tɑnɪk] *n.* 琴湯尼（加奎寧水 quinine water 的杜松子酒）

Chapter
15 博物館

Ⅰ 1. (B) 2. (C) 3. (B)

Ⅱ 1. (B) 2. (C)

❶ 這件明代花瓶是無價之寶。

(A) 是的，博物館的收藏品沒有一件是出售品。

(B) 我相信——它很精緻。

(C) 嗯，我不知道它價值多少錢。

❷ 您可以看到這個鼎細部精心雕琢的匠工。

(A) 噢，那一定很痛。

(B) 一分耕耘，一分收穫。

(C) 哇，很難相信這麼精細的工能在一件這樣小的物品上完成。

Ⅲ 範例解答：

The artifact on the left is a wine jar. It dates from the thirteen century A.D. It is made from clay. It would have been used to store wine before serving. The workmanship is typical of objects like this at the time.

左邊這個工藝品是一個酒甕。它可溯至西元 13 世紀，是由黏土製成的。它可能曾被用來貯藏之後才會取用的酒。這作工是當時這類物品的典型。

exquisite [`ɛkskwɪzɪt] *adj.* 精緻的
intricate [`ɪntrəkɪt] *adj.* 複雜細密的

Chapter
16 道別

| 1. (B)　2. (C)

|| 1. (B)　2. (B)

❶ 我星期一會就新訂單的事與您聯絡。

　　(A) 在那之前，我不會碰它們。

　　(B) 到時候我會等你的消息。

　　(C) 好，我星期一會打電話給您。

❷ 很榮幸您來這裡。

　　(A) 我完全同意！

　　(B) 是我的榮幸。

　　(C) 我也這麼覺得。

||| 範例解答：

I think we can safely say your trip was a good mix of business and pleasure. I'm so happy we were able to reach an understanding about the new directives and resolutions. I'll be in touch next week to work out the details of the final draft.

我想我們可以穩當地說，您這趟行程是工作與娛樂的美妙組合。我很高興我們能就新指示和解決方案達成共識。我下星期會與您聯絡，以擬定最後草案的細節。

directive [dəˋrɛktɪv] *n.* 指令
resolution [ˌrɛzəˋluʃən] *n.* 決議；解決；決心

NOTES

NOTES

國家圖書館出版品預行編目資料

搞定接待英文 = Receiving Guests / Jason
Grenier 作：戴至中譯.——初版.——臺北市：
貝塔, 2005〔民 94〕　　面：　　公分

　ISBN 957-729-531-2（平裝附光碟片）

　1. 英國語言─會話

805.188　　　　　　　　　　　　94013395

搞定接待英文
Receiving Guests

作　　者 / Jason Grenier
總 編 審 / 王復國
譯　　者 / 戴至中
執行編輯 / 邱慧菁

出　　版 / 貝塔出版有限公司
地　　址 / 100 台北市館前路 12 號 11 樓
電　　話 / (02)2314-2525
傳　　真 / (02)2312-3535
郵　　撥 / 19493777 貝塔出版有限公司
客服專線 / (02)2314-3535
客服信箱 / btservice@betamedia.com.tw

總 經 銷 / 時報文化出版企業股份有限公司
地　　址 / 桃園縣龜山鄉萬壽路二段 351 號
電　　話 / (02) 2306-6842

出版日期 / 2008 年 4 月初版二刷
定　　價 / 320 元
ISBN： 957-729-531-2

Receiving Guests
Copyright 2005 by Beta Multimedia Publishing
Published by Beta Multimedia Publishing

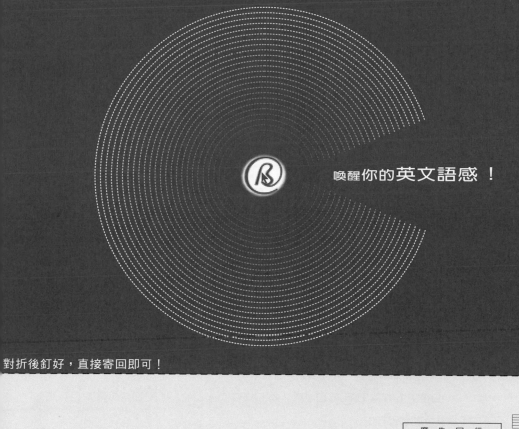

喚醒你的英文語感！

對折後釘好，直接寄回即可！

100 台北市中正區館前路12號11樓

貝塔語言出版 收
Beta Multimedia Publishing

寄件者住址 □□□

謝謝您購買本書！！

貝塔語言擁有最優良之英文學習書籍，為提供您最佳的英語學習資訊，您可填妥此表後寄回（免貼郵票）將可不定期收到本公司最新發行書訊及活動訊息！

姓名：＿＿＿＿＿＿＿＿＿＿＿＿　性別：□男 □女　生日：＿＿＿年＿＿＿月＿＿日

電話：(公)＿＿＿＿＿＿＿＿＿＿(宅)＿＿＿＿＿＿＿＿＿(手機)＿＿＿＿＿＿＿＿＿

電子信箱：＿＿＿＿＿＿＿＿＿＿＿＿＿＿＿＿＿＿＿＿＿

學歷：□高中職含以下 □專科 □大學 □研究所含以上

職業：□金融 □服務 □傳播 □製造 □資訊 □軍公教 □出版

　　　□自由 □教育 □學生 □其他

職級：□企業負責人 □高階主管 □中階主管 □職員 □專業人士

1.您購買的書籍是？＿＿＿＿＿＿＿＿＿＿＿＿＿＿＿＿＿

2.您從何處得知本產品？(可複選)

　　　□書店 □網路 □書展 □校園活動 □廣告信函 □他人推薦 □新聞報導 □其他

3.您覺得本產品價格：

　　　□偏高 □合理 □偏低

4.請問目前您每週花了多少時間學英語？

　　　□ 不到十分鐘 □ 十分鐘以上，但不到半小時 □ 半小時以上，但不到一小時

　　　□ 一小時以上，但不到兩小時 □ 兩個小時以上 □ 不一定

5.通常在選擇語言學習書時，哪些因素是您會考慮的？

　　　□ 封面 □ 內容、實用性 □ 品牌 □ 媒體、朋友推薦 □ 價格□ 其他＿＿＿＿＿

6.市面上您最需要的語言書種類為？

　　　□ 聽力 □ 閱讀 □ 文法 □ 口說 □ 寫作 □ 其他＿＿＿＿＿＿

7.通常您會透過何種方式選購語言學習書籍？

　　　□ 書店門市 □ 網路書店 □ 郵購 □ 直接找出版社 □ 學校或公司團購

　　　□ 其他＿＿＿＿＿＿＿

8.給我們的建議：＿＿＿＿＿＿＿＿＿＿＿＿＿＿＿＿＿＿＿＿＿＿

＿＿＿＿＿＿＿＿＿＿＿＿＿＿＿＿＿＿＿＿＿＿＿＿＿＿＿＿＿

喚醒你的英文語感 ！

Get a Feel for English !

喚醒你的英文語感！

Get a Feel for English !